WITH MY LAZY EYE

Julia Kelly

Quercus

First published in Great Britain in 2009 by

Quercus
21 Bloomsbury Square
London
WC1A 2NS

A CIP catalogue record for this book is available
from the British Library

ISBN 978 1 84724 882 4

10 9 8 7 6 5 4 3 2 1

Printed and bound in Australia by Griffin Press

For my mother and father

Acknowledgements

My sincere thanks go to my publishers, Quercus, in particular Jon Riley and Charlotte Clerk. To my agent, Marianne Gunn O'Connor, for her inspiration, enthusiasm and excellent advice, and to Cormac Kinsella for all his help. To the staff of NCPP for being so supportive, tolerant and flexible over the last three years. Thanks also to Cathal O'Regan for his technical expertise, to Edna and Aidan Jordan for their generosity and to Hugh Hannigan for legal advice. To fellow writers Lorcan Roche, Adrian White, Kusi Okamura and Sheila Mooney for all their guidance and wise words. To John Banville for kindly agreeing to read my work. To my wonderful family and friends who have been so endlessly encouraging and have helped me hold on to my sanity when it was wavering. Thanks especially to the late Roisin Conroy, who first inspired me to write this book, and to Sheila Pratschke, former director of Annaghmakerrig, for helping me to become a writer.

Thanks above all to Charlie, my mentor, muse, soulmate and best friend.

1

Why are there no photos
of baby Bunty?

If you look down through the plughole of the sink in the upstairs bathroom – past gaps in the metal swirl, corroded from years of spat toothpaste, water from a leaking tap and tightly coiled with drenched hair – you'll see a plastic lice comb, lodged at an angle with just an edge exposed, its tiny teeth bleached clean.

I put it there at the age of eight. I pulled it from Mum and pushed it through the overflow hole below Armitage Shanks. I wanted to keep my lice. They were my secret and it was interesting to me to have something living in my hair. I liked to feel the tickle of one as it inched along my eyebrow or hurried its way around my ear. If I was quick enough, I'd catch it and snatch it between my nails, and turn it this way and that under my nose, inspecting it solemnly, somewhat out of focus. Before they were raked out that Sunday night, we'd been happily cohabiting my head.

Mum hummed on our way to the bathroom that evening, as she does when she moves from one place to another, or when she goes to answer the front door. Or when something has gone wrong like her cheese soufflé not rising. Then she'll hum a different, louder hum as she scrapes the hot eggy mixture into the bin.

Up the stairs goes little me; I'm as sleepy as can be. Loud hum, soft hum, as a slipper pounded each stair. Up I went too, following her and the Frog, his bony bruised legs like strips of melded plasticine gripping around her soft centre.

I climbed two steps at a time behind them, pulling at the loose banister. *And how many times have I told you not to?* The sock in my left shoe had slipped down past the heel and my skin was sticking to the shiny leather inner.

Mum pulled both of us out of our ankle-deep, luke-warm bath prematurely. Someone had done a number two. It bobbed about in the turbulence we created getting out. Her hands holding me around the chest were cold; water snaked along her fingers, which were greasy pink like she'd been smearing butter on a goosepimply old chicken. That's when she tried to comb my hair.

Nothing felt nice that evening to begin with. It was Sunday, only one more sleep till Monday, which meant school. Sunday also meant *The Muppet Show*.

My father would join us in the playroom for this half-hour each week. When we heard him coming we'd jump out of the bookshelves we had fashioned into boats or burst through the cushions of our secret homemade dens. Once he had settled in a chair with its stuffing pulled out and found a space around our lives for his Jameson's and jiggly ice, he'd sniff and say,

'Has someone let that damned cat in again?' We'd sniff too, bubbly snot under our noses, and say we couldn't smell anything.

My father laughed at the two old judges and 'Pigs in Space' with his mouth thrown so wide I could see two strings of saliva near his throat, like a puppet mouth, a muppet mouth, as well as some stuck liquorice and silver shapes on grey like the sparkles on the rocks on Sandymount Strand.

I sat on the floor beside the television because of my lazy eye, and cried. I cried about school and about having no friends. The more my father laughed, the more I cried. But the more I cried, the less anyone listened and the less I could make out what Miss Piggy was saying. The playroom was steamy through my pig-pink eyes, the way it went when Mum had forgotten our fish fingers on the grill.

My mother was too busy in the kitchen to watch TV with us. When she came in on a search for dirty dishes, Ollie sat forward with his hands over his ears. We all wished she'd go back to the washing up because of the cold coming through the door she'd left open, and because she was talking over the best bits of the show. Mum likes to talk about what she sees on television the way she would if she were driving by interesting scenery on the road to Brittas Bay. She looked at the screen through the corner of one eye. The other one watched my father. If something made her laugh she would give him a sidelong glance to check if he felt the same way.

I got myself to sleep that Sunday night and other nights by banging my head against my bedroom wall. This gave me a big hairstyle and made a large chalky hole, which I could hide things like Playmen and Monopoly pieces in.

As I rocked in bed, I liked to think about my favourite clothes and me inside them. But the me in my head wouldn't have brown hair; it would be yellow, like Charlie's from *Willy Wonka and the Chocolate Factory*. I would be thin, so that you could see my ribs even when I wasn't breathing in, and I would be a boy. My three best things were:

1. My purple corduroy cap that Mr McNellis gave me for my eighth birthday, just before he had his heart attack. I hadn't seen it for a while; maybe it was in the clothes basket in the downstairs bathroom beneath all that ancient table linen and underwear and slips.

2. My *Man from Atlantis* swimming togs which were orange, tight and to the knee. With my flippers on, arms flat by my sides, I'd twist underwater in the shallow end of the pool, pretending to rescue people like the girl who couldn't swim in the red Polyotters. Before I went under I'd have to memorize where my victims were – Doctor Nugent said I might be allergic to chlorine so until Mum bought me some new goggles I had to swim with my eyes closed.

3. The Frog's verruca socks, which I teamed with a
   pair of red-rimmed Y-fronts with pictures of soldiers
   on them and a matching polyester vest. I like to
   wear this outfit when practising my running – on
   your marks, get set, and up the laneway behind the
   blue garage as fast as I could.

But none of these things had my name sewn into any
part of them, like Oscar's and Patsy's did. They went to
boarding school and had their own pairs of socks and
gym kits and washbags and suitcases, all with their first
and second names embroidered in. They had particular
things they had to do at particular times of the day.

We were told to play together while our mothers
collected for the Homeless Girls Society. I wanted to be
adopted by them, to have a father like theirs, living in
America, as well as a man from up the road who sometimes stayed over and bought them Sherbet Dips, and
a mother who noticed tiny things about them, who
knew how much they weighed, which cereal each
preferred, whose socks belonged to whom.

I remembered being in a cage on a mountainside,
naked and covered in mud. There was a berry between
my feet and when I bent to pick it up, the berry became
a bluebottle. Then the bluebottle was gone but I could
still hear it near my ear, and when its noise stopped I
knew it had landed on some part of me to explore.
Bubbling bottle pops, hoots and burbles, and slippery

gumboots on rocks tumbled down a waterfall and away from me. My head was hot and damp and I wanted to tumble with them, but I didn't know who to shout to because I couldn't see what voice belonged to which feet. I pushed my left hand through the bars and drew in dried mud with a stick until it snapped.

There's a photograph of my older sister, Pie, in that playpen at a picnic in Wicklow. And when I ask Mum why there are no baby pictures of me when there's a pictorial shrine to Pie and the Frog, it was because I was born in the winter when it was dark, she'll say, or because I didn't like my picture being taken, or because photos just weren't something we were thinking about at the time.

That I was an antisocial middle child, with a bucket-shaped face, left-handed, lazy-eyed, mildly brain-damaged (as a result of repeated, self-inflicted blows to the head), lice-infested, chronically self-absorbed bed-wetter with vile and murderous tendencies wasn't mentioned.

I tried to kill the pallid Frog by forcing a Pete's Peanut up his nose when he was three. He turned that colour he went when he was having an Incredible Sulk or was on the potty – raw pink like luncheon meat – but he didn't growl or thrash his feet; he made a thin whistling sound as if he were asleep. He went away for a bit, but he came home again with a new trolley full of bricks. My father sat with the Frog on the playroom floor and using the bricks they built a fortress around them.

But I didn't kill Granny. I know it looked a little suspicious because I was the one who found her. My father didn't blame me when I told him that she wasn't moving in her bed, but I know what he must have been thinking and I bet he said something to Mum. Granny was fine at the Christmas party we'd had twenty-four hours earlier. She was wearing a blue twinset that I'd seen before, with her handbag dangling at her elbow like Minnie Mouse. Under her arm was a bottle of TK Lemonade for us. I remember her face looked red but I thought that was because she'd just taken something out of the oven. Yak Yak Yak, she said as she picked up a dirty tea towel.

I knocked on her bedroom window the next morning with her newspaper. She'd been living underneath us since her balance had got bad. Then I let myself in and called out along the hall and again outside the bedroom door; I was afraid to open it in case she was in the middle of putting on a girdle or peeling plasters off her bunions.

She didn't look at me or move when I came in – her eyes were staring at the ceiling. She had a hairnet on and she'd put that powdery stuff all over her cheeks and forehead, but she'd forgotten to do the two sore bits at the top of her nose, at that place where glasses sit, and the grey fluffy part above her upside-down mouth, along the lines where lipstick slid.

I didn't know what death looked like but I thought that dead hands and arms would be spread out, like Jesus on the Cross, or like people in films after they've been shot. Granny's hands, all waxy and bunched, were gripping the bedclothes. Blue veins criss-crossed under her brown-spotted skin. Her fingernails were thick like toenails and curled at the edges, and though they were coated in cherry, I could see soft toffee stuff underneath. Her legs were crossed from the knee, the way she liked to cross them in front of her on a pouffe when she was watching the races at Leopardstown on the black and white television.

The travel alarm clock was ticking and a *Reader's Digest* bookmark stuck out of the Bible on the bedside table. Walking shoes – royal blue, bunion-shaped at the sides to fit her bunion-feet, and with a slipped Scholl insole inside each – were waiting under her bed.

A funnel of sunlight stretched from the window to a painting of Jesus above Granny's head. Inside the light were dancing diamonds of dust, Granny's dust. Dust to dust. Was her soul leaving when I opened the door? Was she stranded in limbo because of me, above her bed in bits of dust? Granddad was on his horse watching us from the mantelpiece. Maybe he was waiting to take her away or maybe she'd already gone off with Jesus.

Granny had changed but her smell was the same: a mix of brandy, Cussons talc, damp dog on a pink bath mat and twenty cigarettes from a packet of gold, the same gold as the Terry's All Gold she'd bought me when I'd burnt my toe on the gas heater. I was afraid to touch her; I didn't want to give her a fright. If

Granny had gone where was her soul? Maybe it was searching for her suitcase in Herbert Park pond, that's where she thought the robbers might have thrown it after they'd stolen it from under her bed and used it to carry away all her favourite things, like the squirrel salt cellar and the two silver candlesticks. And when the Frog fell into the pond by mistake, did his blue boots touch the edge of Granny's suitcase at the bottom? Is that where Granny floated now, deep and silent, in her nightie, with purple tubes like trapped worms along the backs of her knees, through mossy undergrowth, green water, twigs and leaves and spawn?

I tried to cry because that's what people do when they stand beside bodies, but I didn't feel sad. I felt oddly excited. I started to laugh. It was me who found Granny! It was my big bit of news. I wouldn't even have to knock on my father's study door; I could run right in with such an important thing to say.

It wasn't the right time to die because my birthday was still to come and she was going to get me a Space Hopper and because Mum was up in Belfast buying her a cassette recorder for Christmas. And if someone looked through my bedroom window at the exact moment that I was applying blusher to my cheeks on the day of Granny's funeral they would have seen me smile and they might have thought there was something a bit fishy about that. But I read in Mum's copy of *Good Housekeeping* that blusher should be applied to the apples of your cheeks and that the best way to find these apples is to smile. Mum suggested that I might want to look like a proper girl on that day. Then she hummed as she folded the cleaned sheet from Granny's bed and put it back into the hot press.

2

Downstairs upstairs

I imagined myself into the painting of the storm. It was where I went when things were going wrong. Not out on the slushy street with the bent-over men and women in shawls struggling to move forwards in the squall, but in the house at the front of the painting. There were no lights in the windows or smoke from its chimney; I painted these in with my mind. Inside where it would be warm with burning wood, I'd climb a ladder to bed through smudgy candlelight, in my long johns and bare feet, and listen to doors slam, wind buffeting the windows, sleet pelting the roof.

The painting hadn't been hung there for me. It hadn't been hung at all, but wedged between the bookshelves above my bed along with other things for which no home could be found like the old warming pan my mother got when Granny died and the statue of the Virgin Mary, missing her head.

I'd been helping Mum with eclairs for the dinner party, breaking chocolate into a saucepan while she stirred with a wooden spoon. The spoon was in her mouth when my father came in carrying the table linen he'd collected from the Swastika Laundry. 'You really shouldn't be eating that, pet,' he said. I agreed with him; I hated when she licked things and put them straight back in the bowl. Mum said she'd eat what she bloody well liked.

She swore more often since her mother died, whereas my father was enjoying the peace. Granny talked too much when she was alive, the way old people do when you invite them over for lunch.

Happy occasions such as Christmas and dinner parties often made my parents swear, and the hours before them were fiercely tense in our house. By the time the first guests had arrived – always too early – my parents were generally not talking to each other. Aside from worrying about what would happen to us if they broke up or the threat of being asked to vacuum the hall, parties were exciting events: the fridge was fat with chocolate mousses in frosted bowls and plates wrapped in tinfoil and not to be touched, the house was warmer than usual with the heating being allowed on, there was the prospect of presents from godparents to look forward to, but, above all, was the thrill of being allowed into the good rooms.

Though ours was a six-bedroomed Victorian pile, we inhabited only the antechambers and servants' quarters for eleven months of the year. On special occasions and on Christmas Day the keys to the good rooms were procured by my father from his secret hiding place, allowing us to venture into the vast, high-ceilinged reception rooms, and certain cold, unnavigated rooms at the top of the house, where overseas guests would be brought to sleep.

My father's wireless fuzzed from where it was lying face down on the bedroom carpet, angled to pick up the Third Programme. It was playing that spooky old harpsichord music he liked, the sort that made me think of dark palaces and furious kings.

With a snort he got up from where he'd been kneeling in black evening socks and Jockey briefs, the texture of the Persian rug imprinted on each kneecap. 'Doorbell!' he roared, establishing the cause of the interference, to no particular and all members of his family at the same time.

He twiddled the tuner, touring through Hilversum, Oslo and Radio Luxembourg before winding it back to Handel again, and laid two centre sheets of an old *Irish Times* on the rug, the first lengthways, the second on top of it but in the opposite direction like a protective cross. He folded his shirt sleeves to above the loose skin of his elbows and marshalled what he'd need for the job: Kiwi shoe polish in tan, a horsehair brush, the bristles so worn in the middle that you could see through to the pores in the wood, a leather buffer and half an underpant for application.

He selected a particular pair of brogues from ten identical sets lined up under a row of suits, hung in the wardrobe like limbless ghosts in a queue, and shoved a hand into an elderly inner. He bobbed his head in time to the music as he worked polish into leather, lifting the shoe glove-style and turning it in the air; the damp circles on its base like age rings on a tree. 'Oh, Christmas!' he cursed when a lump of polish fell onto the rug, his weak eyes bulging to locate it before it smudged.

He kept his head still with the effort he employed for buffing. The three strands of silver hair combed across his pate fell over his face as he polished, the way they did when we were smacked. Task complete, he sat back on his hunkers and paused to admire his work.

'Ach! Doorbell, for crying out loud!' he bellowed on his way to the bathroom to shave.

Mum watched the choux pastry shells not rising through the oven window. Something wasn't right, their consistency looked wrong. She opened the door, stuck a finger into the mix, licked it, then closed the door again. Mrs Beecham's recipe for profiteroles would have to be double-checked.

The doorbell had been ringing for so long now that it had ceased being a single sound, but had split into a series of separate little tunes, like an orchestra in rehearsal, each busily playing their particular parts. Mum wouldn't have heard it at all if she hadn't opened the kitchen door when she did, to put the cat back out.

Pulling her apron off she went through the hall, humming a doorbell sort of chime purposefully loud to assure whoever was behind the front door that not only was she on her way but that everyone in our house was in high good form.

The mortified guests – Mr and Mrs McClean who had just moved into number 27 and were only being invited because the Hamptons had pulled out – had spent the previous few minutes trying to unstick the doorbell. 'That ruddy thing!' said Mum, whacking it with the base of her hand. Out it popped and in out of the cold they came.

Early guests were abandoned in the drawing-room. Carrying a steak and kidney pie on her way up to the Hostess Trolley in the dining-room next door, Mum tried to cajole us in to welcome them: 'Will you not go in and say hello?'

'Mu-um!' Ollie whined, on his way to the playroom to watch *Top of the Pops* with some cheese on toast and a milk-moustache mouth, cross that she'd made this suggestion within probable earshot of the guests, but knowing at the same time that she was too addled to insist upon anything.

'Honestly, you'd swear I was asking you to ...' she said, in that stiff smiling voice she uses when overheard, trailing off as she tried to count place settings, her right eye travelling towards her nose the way it does when she's preoccupied.

The husband and wife in the drawing-room didn't have anything new to say to each other so he looked at family photos and paintings with his hands behind his back, lifting his glasses and bending forwards periodically to better check some inscription or date. She sat at the edge of the sofa, closed-legged and upright, the way she never normally would, trying not to crease her skirt, with that expression that she keeps for parties – a fixed look of pleasant expectation towards the door. Left alone a little longer she snatched out her compact, face contorted the way it changes when it sees itself in the mirror, bracelets a-jingle as she flicked a hand through her hair. Then, with the swift adoption of a bow-legged stance she yanked her tights up while her husband quietly eased some trapped gas from his system in the far corner of the room.

Billows of vapour travelled out through the wet lattice window of the bathroom – over the flat roof with its cracked ice puddles, leaf-jammed gutters and one of my father's handkerchiefs tied to a naked Action Man – before freezing into the December night. The sky was deep velvet and empty but for the distant red lights of a plane, a spattering of stars and some floating white flumps from the striped towers of the cloud factory on South Wall. A layer of frost spread over the leaves and sticks on the stiff rectangles of grass in the front garden; at the back of the house, the elongated shadow of the kitchen window stretched as far as the rubber tyre swing beneath the Scots pine. Little puffs of air escaped from the mouths of men as they climbed the front steps in galoshes, directing each other as they parked, getting that first joke in quick. Steam from the lifted lid of a pot on the cooker, from the scorching water whistling through the kitchen sink tap. Steam too from the hot chocolate Ollie slurped under a blanket he'd dragged down from upstairs, his eyes all the while roaming his *Tintin* comic.

I could hear Mr Malone's wheezy cough in the hall. What starts out as a chuckle had lately developed into full-blown emphysema, a five-minute stomach-turning hack, finished off with a spluttering up of chewy phlegm. I tried not to make him laugh. Doctor Long had cracked the joke, he always laughed loudest at himself. Granny's former bridge partner, Mrs MacDermot, was down there too. Old Mrs MacDermot was a contrary old soul, particularly when it came to her daughter, Stephanie, who was her antithesis. 'Have you not met Stephanie?' Mum always says, 'Stephanie's great, she's big and bouncy.' Bigger and bouncier than ever, she had just produced a baby girl whom she had christened Poppy.

'Only Blacks give their babies made-up names,' said Mrs MacDermot. Mr Malone cleared his throat. Doctor Long moved away.

My mother was speaking to the McCleans in a strange new accent – theirs. What we traditionally referred to as the 'garage' had become a roomier-sounding 'gar*auche*'. She had a way of altering her voice to suit the person she was speaking to. Our Chinese gardener, Chang Lee, she addressed in broken English, enunciating each word in a slow shout and with an array of hand gestures the deaf would find excessive.

Mrs Scott Hamilton sounded silly already. I wondered when she'd start using the vase Didi Malone bought Mum as an ashtray for her cheroots. It came jammed into a box from Brown Thomas, but we saw the same vase at O'Connor's Hardware last Saturday, reduced to two for five pounds. Posterior in the air, she travelled through the hall, like a hen, in search of the loo.

And then there were three or four voices together and someone must have said something hilarious. Great howls and shrieks of laughter, pops of bottles and bubbles, the clink of champagne glasses, a freshly lit cigar. Pine needles and perfume and faces too hot, men tightly fitted in their shirts and their skins, the women all jingle flutter flatter. All bosoms and legs and Absolutely! Haw haw haw. Mr McClean on the fringes of the group, still a little gassy.

But something was going to go wrong. A denture might come free in the middle of a story or there could be a fight like last time about whether the Swiss were a good or bad race. Doctor Long might come and sit with us in the playroom with his shirt poking through his opened fly. Or Didi Malone could walk in on Doctor Long's wife while she hovered over the toilet in the unlockable downstairs bathroom trying not to catch our germs.

With the inevitable delayed for as long as politely possible, having not wanted to throw a party in the first place, my father went downstairs – a last thunderous purge of his nose along the way – quickening his step for the final flight to portray enthusiasm and so that his guests would hear him as he made his entry.

Rooms changed when my father entered them, as though the lights had suddenly been switched on. People stood up, women fiddled with their hair, conversation became animated, eyes wandered to where he was.

Doctor Long shouted something, there was an abrupt clap, followed by a spontaneous round of applause. A lower voice – my father's witty retort – then chortles like bubbles travelling up and down windpipes, like ice cubes and lemon tumbling around a glass.

On school mornings I'd watch him take the front steps, nimble, quick, and stride out along the gravel, off to a job I knew nothing about in the city. Sometimes he would disappear into a long black car. His driver, Mr Barry – who I dreamt of being because he was a man, and alternatively of being married to because he looked so smart and serious in his uniform and flat cap – holding the door open and relieving my father of his briefcase.

I pictured great halls and wood-panelled rooms, books lining the walls and high ceilings, my father at a window formulating ideas and solutions to things, or seated behind a vast mahogany desk, glaring over his glasses, dictating to a shorthand typist. People would neaten themselves in the corridor outside, and hesitate before knocking on his door.

Now that my father was downstairs, Mum could go up and get changed. When I heard her coming I climbed off the banister I'd been scaling and hid behind the velvet curtains in their bedroom in the mouse mask I'd worn for the school play. Mum had cut the eyes out wonky, one was higher up than the other and they were both too small. The only way to see where I was going was to look out through the bottom of it.

Mum sat at her dressing table pulling dead dyed hairs

from a brush. With eyes shut she sprayed Elnett about to make her hairstyle set. Once she'd painted and powdered her face, she stepped into some tights and jangled about her wardrobe for a suitable outfit to wear.

She stood before the mirror in her ballerina pose – the one she always uses to look at herself. Head up, shoulders back, big breath in. One leg stretched far out in front of her, an arm by her side, the other held at an angle, hand flexed – Mum never seems sure about what to do with her spare hand. Her feet looked too small for the rest of her, like she'd borrowed them from somebody else. She wore a salmon-coloured crimplene trouser suit with a pea-green waistcoat beneath. Something was missing. She rummaged about in her drawer for a scarf. A scarf finishes an outfit off, she says. Back in front of the mirror she flung it movie-star style across her chest.

My eyelashes flicked like trapped flies behind the mask. My breath was making the cardboard wet and the rubber band was too tight against my ears. 'You little monkey,' Mum said when she saw the curtains move. 'Will you not come down and say hello?' I didn't need to answer; she wouldn't wait for a reply. She was gone, leaving just her scent behind: the warm flowery smell that meant she was going somewhere without us. I trailed back out to the landing.

I hadn't wanted to be a mouse. I'd wanted to be one of the three kings. I envied their exotic costumes and had learnt all their lines. At the purple curtain I queued behind them in their tinfoil crowns and cloaks with the other bit-part players: the clouds, the blades of grass, the trees. The cardboard set oscillated as we took our positions on stage to the raw sound of the upright piano Mrs French played. She held her eyes on us as she struck the keys; her mouth stretched huge prompting the words of songs we'd been rehearsing for weeks.

When I'd tired of reciting everyone else's lines, I pulled off my mouse mask and set it on top of my head. I scanned the room for my parents: it was hazy out there beyond the white stage lights. Someone had a cough, people were shifting in their seats to get comfortable, some small commotion was going on at the entrance door; it opened, closed and opened again. There was Mum near the front – I waved when I saw her. The Frog had his head on her shoulder and looked asleep in his zipped-up anorak. But where was my father? Everyone else was there to see our play, even the mother who had three weeks to live and no hair.

Through the banisters I watched the Frog. He knew how cute he looked struggling upstairs under the weight of the guests' winter coats, his milky skin and shoulder-length white hair poking from that itchy green polo neck Mrs McCabe knitted for him last year. My father promised to pay him five pence if he collected coats and brought them up to the spare room. With his rash-wrinkled skin and malnourished frame, the Frog was always being given things, which he carefully catalogued and indexed and saved.

Pie baby-stepped through the hall towards the drawing-room, in her new jersey dress and white tights with a tear in the knee, a bottle of wine secured under each arm. Her nostrils flared as she sucked her lips in with effort and her stubby pigtails bounced as she moved. Sometimes they would do gymnastic routines together for the guests, Pie thumping across the hall carpet in her leotard – mottled legs unaccustomed to exposure, the first suggestion of breasts – cart-wheeling towards her poorly matched partner bracing himself to catch her mid-flight. If that bit went OK, Pie would balance the Frog on her feet in the air. 'Ah Pie! You'll crease him!' my father would say as everyone enthused and clapped.

If I timed it right no one would spot me on my way down to the playroom. I was terrified of being forced into a room full of adults. I never knew who was who, who was standing where, what I should say, who had seen me, who was smiling and waving at me to come over, whether I could slip out again because no one had noticed me at all.

I'd lost my voice, the way I did every Christmas, which was why I had to be on guard. Traditionally this was when my father liked to record me reciting nursery rhymes in front of his friends. Bent on one knee to get down to my size, he would hold his Dictaphone by my mouth, his lips parted in expectation. After the first line of 'Georgie Porgie' there were no words at all, just sporadic high-pitched squeaks, just my mouth opening and closing like a fish and the sound of my father and a hazy assortment of high heels and tights and suit jackets above me.

I took off my mask and pulled my face into a long stretch to make my eyes open wide, like someone pretending to be English and posh. China blue, my father said, when I was standing on the bench in the kitchen that day. I tried to picture china blue – the colour of the teacups at Uncle Pat's house? But my father didn't know about my secret trick. My eyes weren't blue at all; they were small and grey and one was bigger than the other. It was only when I looked out of windows that they changed colour and got bright and see-through.

I was afraid the guests would notice that my eyes didn't match. That I couldn't make my lazy one look at them even when I tried, and that I couldn't help it if my bad eye went off, right over their shoulders when they spoke, out of the window and away.

I imagined stretching that knobbly wart on Mr Barnham's chin, as far as it could go, then letting it ping back just to see what everyone would say. 'Absolutely divine' would become 'Absolutely disgusting!' And the way they'd say disgusting would be like this: diz ghust ing, the way Percy the gardener said it when the *Blue Peter* garden was vandalized.

As I snuck past the drawing-room, I could hear my father telling Genevieve a joke. Something to do with the King being dead – they were still going on about that. I squinted around the open door, with my back pressed against it, private-detective style. His hand touched her bracelet as she laughed, all lipsticky sweet. He laughed too and held on to her arm, making out that he needed to just to stay upright.

Mum was back in the kitchen biting her bottom lip as she beat the new profiterole mix. She told me what she was doing the way she does when you come into a room that she's in. 'You must beat it briskly, it's all in the wrist.' A piece of hair fell over her face as she beat; she pinched her fingers round it and put it back in place. It fell over her face again, but this time she left it there, held on to the bowl and beat harder.

All the guests had gone but the air was still thick with the mix of cooking, Chanel and cigars. Someone hadn't liked the steak and kidney pie; they'd scraped it to the edge of their plate and had covered it with a napkin. An unopened box of After Eights lay on top of a discarded purple scarf.

Into the dining-room I crept, over to the sideboard and down to the cupboard that looked locked but was secretly open. I put my hand in the box of Lemon's sweets, felt around for the ones I wanted and washed them down with some soda water. Father Christmas was laughing on the front with silver snow all around him and sleighs flying through a purple sky.

On my way back to bed I saw a strip of yellow light coming from under the drawing-room door. Someone must have forgotten to switch the Christmas tree lights off. I snuck in to see if any of the guests had left presents for me.

When I slid my hand under the branches there was a sudden kerfuffle. My father was sitting on the sofa in the dark with Genevieve; she seemed delighted to see me and slapped her hand down in the space that spread swiftly between them.

My father liked me best at these times – when his friends were with him or after dinner parties when he was happy. I loved these times too – having his attention and being let stay up late. But he didn't want me there that night. 'Ah Bunty! What is the meaning of this?' he said. His accent was peculiar, like an American's. Words were skating off his teeth and his eyes weren't focusing on me. 'Back to bed this instant!'

The door handle of our bedroom bounced a bit later. 'Hi!' my father said, rolling backwards then forwards again. Pie didn't move in her bed. He had his wireless in one hand, a Jameson's in the other; his wet eyes making him look upset. He bent down to me with his smell of coal-tar soap and gave me lots of little quick kisses on the forehead, interrupted by a hiccup.

3

Belief and beyond

My father disappeared with the best deckchair, the black and cream Bovril flask and a shape like a butterfly on his trousers where he must have sat on something. 'Who wanted egg?' said Mum, sounding tired. She was sitting on a rug on the ground between chairs, her legs stretched out on either side of the picnic basket, like a toy doll in charge, trying to exert some authority over us but knowing that chaos would reign now that my father had gone. We swarmed around her, pulling at the things we had packed an hour earlier, bickering with each other about who got what first. Out came the pink ham, two packets of EasiCheese Singles, some sliced tomatoes in tinfoil.

Picnics were always unsettling. I'd start out in good humour but some great injustice, like not being allowed a third packet of Tayto or the irritation of Mum breathing over my food, Pie pushing against me, the insects snooping around, would inevitably darken my mood.

Mum passed Pie the MiWadi to mind – there was hardly any left since I'd knocked it over, flowing under all of our seats, presenting my father with the perfect excuse to escape. Pie wedged it between her nettle-rash knees and turned the cap extra tight. Then she opened a packet of Tayto, sprinkled handfuls over her Spam, Bovril and salad-cream sandwich, and scrunched everything together.

I hated mixed-up things; I was happy with banana and butter, but I had to eat it swiftly so there would still be some sweets left – Ollie was already rooting for his Wagon Wheel while Mum tried lazily to refine his home-scissored hair. He ate some custard so fast once that it came straight back out in two lines from his nose.

We were permanently hungry but were never taken to McDonalds like everyone else and had to survive on homemade food. At an early age I developed a taste for rubber – hot-water bottles, elastic bands, tennis shoes – but what I liked best of all was Aunt Maureen's leather car seats. I liked to lick and chew the headrests. I took a large bite from one once. In the same way as there's never enough biscuit on a cheesecake, there was too little leather, too much foamy stuff underneath. Frog was the only pernickety eater in the family, refusing all but Denny sausage rolls which he only liked the pastry parts of. These he ate at a little table on his own with his back to the rest of us, to prevent him from getting indigestion.

We were a plastic cup short because someone had trapped a wasp; it was under a seat in the upside-down snare, banging around with its shadow, making tiny 'tisk' sounds. Mum swallowed her oxtail soup from the flask-top, shook it out, splashing her shoes, and handed it to me to use. Little oxtails swam around in the orange as I poured and it looked the wrong colour to begin with in the brown flask-top, it tasted too weak, too warm.

I pulled a hair from the banana mix in my mouth; my tongue found it first, twisted up in the bread. I fiddle-fingered it out, gagging the longer it grew and cleaning it unintentionally between my lips as it came, sludgy bits of banana stuck to silver-grey.

'Oh for Pete's sake! It's only a hair.'

I swivelled into a sulk. The woman behind me was spindly, with a scarf tied under her chin. She looked organized and cross, like a teacher. There was a boy in a blazer beside her and between them on a special stool was a proper plastic lunch box. The sandwiches in the lunch box weren't in the wrapper from the sliced pan; they were shaped like little triangles and covered in cling film. And if they were still hungry they had a Babybel cheese and a mini Swiss Roll each.

I wondered what we looked like to them? I wished Mum would bend at the knee when she needed to get things from the picnic basket instead of keeping her legs straight and her bum in the air. She was talking too loud on purpose, just in case the people around us might be interested in what she had to say. But they weren't listening to her.

We were up near the front with all the dying people and presidents and priests and TV cameras and VIPs, because my father was important and maybe also because of me, because I couldn't see properly. Megaphones crackled as more and more people came, pushing against me to get organized with their transistor radios and squeaking wheelchairs, exposing tucked thermal vests in huge nylon pants as they bent, airing musty old indoor smells when they finally sat down sighing. Everyone was thanking the Lord about this and that and weren't we lucky with the weather, and asking us if we'd mind awfully moving up a little bit. 'Oh! not at all, of course yes, sorry yes!' Mum shunting me along with her hips, saying something about Dunkirk and not looking at where I might be going.

I scanned the crowd for my father; I couldn't see anything clearly. I couldn't see the air-raid shelter near Palmerstown Park when he lifted me up against a wall and told me to look over the top. I pretended I could, because I knew my father thought this was just the sort of thing small children would find interesting. I was too heavy in his arms; as he held me round the waist they trembled. I wanted to ask what an air-raid shelter looked like in the first place. But he put me down again before I could, because it was getting dark and Pie and the Frog still needed a turn.

A million heads swarmed behind me like an endless cobblestone road. Close up in colour and detail and shape, then diffusing and blurring into one great grey borderless thing, swelling outwards and down, as far as the deer grazing beyond tiny Christmas trees. I wanted to shout, to hear my voice travel and fall, to run over everyone's heads. It was called devotion when men crumpled over their umbrellas muttering things, when nuns knelt with their tangled rosary beads. A man from St Johns Ambulance fed water to a woman who'd been sick in her handbag. White flowers fluttered in the arms of an Irish dancing girl, ankle-socked, knees together, a last sticky-licked hanky wipe to her cheek. Blurred bodies behind railings looked ahead. I bet they were wondering what was so special or so wrong about me, that I should be five rows from the front. But everyone wore a badge, they had theirs too, which told you who you were and where you were meant to be.

Then there was clapping, like rain on the playroom roof, and everyone got up in a rush. Mum's cardigan slid off the back of her chair, milky tea spilt, flies flew. When he first came on stage with all those sinister bishops and cardinals, I waved my yellow flag. We all did, even the adults, holding theirs between their thumbs and fingers like daisies, which looked a bit silly I thought. 'Let us pray,' and down we all sat again. I tilted forward until the back legs of my deckchair lifted off the ground, fitting my face into the circle-shaped space between a woman wearing a brown hat like a Hazelnut Swirl, and the man beside her who'd forgotten his socks, his heels like turnips wedged into shoes.

Being around crowds of old people scared me. I was worried that one of them would collapse and be carried off the way Granny had been or that I'd have to perform that manoeuvre I'd heard about if they choked on their teeth. Someone might wet themselves like the lady I'd seen outside Donnybrook church, crouched in a side-door, handbag twisted around her fingers, tights pulled down, flowery dress hitched up, Mum telling me not to stare as a stream of wee travelled towards me.

Mum asked if I could see properly but all I could make out was a cream thing with missing feet fluttering far away over hats and flying grey hairs, dangling about in the wind like the plastic statue of Jesus Mr McCabe had tied to the rear-view mirror of his car. I couldn't hear what he was saying and the wind was blowing his voice over our heads, down the valley all the way over to Car Park E, where there was no one listening.

Why couldn't God just appear if He was there that day? What was the big secret? And what was in that secret box on the altar – the one that was always locked? What happened in those rooms backstage and behind the curtains of confessional boxes, which people came out from crying? Why were there great purple covers over everything? Why did I have a headless statue of the Virgin Mary above my bed? Why had no one thrown her in the bin if she was broken? Or was that a mortal sin?

The Hazelnut Swirl kept moving and getting in my way and the front bar of the deckchair was digging into my legs. I swung back, too far in the other direction, but recovered well. Mum turned to me with her eyebrows arched like two caterpillars about to have a fight, she looked sad and looked forward again and rejoined her hands. I hated the way religion did that to people's faces; it meant there was no chance of getting their attention.

Everything was moving too slowly. I made a rabbit hop along the cement with the shadow of two fingers, and up the tartan rug of the woman in the wheelchair beside me, who smelt of vegetable soup. Trying not to think about how horrible it would feel to bite her rug between my teeth made me think about it again and again. With my finger and thumb I made a gun, slipping it into its holster when a guard passed by, in case he saw its shadow and thought I was getting ready to assassin-ate the Pope when he waved at us from his mobile. The choir sang 'Be Not Afraid' and I swam away and back into my head. Back to what had happened that morning, from the very beginning again.

I'd ridden my Chopper down to the Cash Stores to get some ham for our picnic, zigzagging in and out of the white stripes in the centre of the road, leaping over ramps, Evel Knievel, and doing little wheelies on the safe smooth bits. Then back in the saddle and no hands for longer than I'd done before, long enough to do a quick sign of the cross at the church. A low, sharp turn round the corner before the bridge, knee nearly grazing ground, motorbike-racer style, and fast as anything for the final straight, off the saddle, head over handlebars, speeding through hills of swept up leaves.

I had to keep stopping on my way back; the plastic bag I'd looped round the handlebars was swinging too much with the sweaty ham and getting caught in the spokes. But I didn't look annoyed; I was still thinking about Mr Brown and the joke we'd had when I'd asked him how much the penny chews were.

'Hello there!'

I scrunched up my eyes to see Billie coming towards me. She was wearing a leather jacket and smiling. I dismounted in that way you can if you're an experienced rider, one leg over the top, quick as anything, and still cycling for a bit, balanced on one pedal. It sometimes went wrong, which hurt, but that morning it worked out perfectly.

I told her we were off to visit the Pope and she said how exciting that would be for me. I mentioned just in passing where we would be sitting, and asked her what row she was in. She said she wasn't going, that she was looking forward to spending the day walking around an empty city. Then she smiled at me again, and I could see some white chewing gum between her teeth.

I was pleased with our conversation because I didn't stutter once. Not even when I started that sentence with 'Y', when I said, 'You know, because of Dad being a VIP.' And I was extra pleased that she saw me in the outfit I had on: my green army sweater with patches on the elbows and shoulders, my white aeroplane T-shirt underneath – you couldn't see it, but it was the one with the plastic blue plane in the middle that stuck out like it was real. I had my new jeans on with the shopping list in the back pocket which I knew made me look good in an American sort of way, and blue Converse runners; the lace was broken on the right one so I'd had to tie it very far down to keep it on. I liked that they made me look as if I'd been through a lot.

The only thing wrong was the colour of my Chopper. It was red; silver was what I'd asked for. Mum said they weren't making the silver ones any more but there was a picture of one on the back of the brand new box of Rice Krispies, which you could enter a competition to win if you collected fifty tokens and explained why you love Rice Krispies in less than ten words.

My hair was doing just the right thing. I'd woken with my fringe sticking up at the front, which made me look sweaty and tough, and I pictured my neck being downy and brown like a boy's. As we stood there chatting about this and that, I could feel the sun warming and browning it even more, making the little lines of hair on my neck whiter so there'd be a lovely difference between the two. I was looking at Billie through the sun so I knew my eyes would be light and blue, and the middle of my right one would have shrunk and stopped looking all swollen and strange like David Bowie's. When our conversation was over I took off as fast as I could. As soon as I'd steadied myself I sat back and cycled with one hand, but I'm not sure if she saw that bit.

Billie was my Art Appreciation teacher at school. She was different from the others; she sat on the table in class with her boots on a turned-around chair, and her pink Sasperillas were so tight that you could make out the shape of her downstairs. When she told us about Giotto drawing a perfect freehand circle for a pope, she opened her eyes wide, perfect-circle wide, and squinted them into little slits when she talked about Caravaggio having murdered a man. I loved it when she picked on me and made me stay late after class, even if it was because I'd made everyone laugh when my legs got stuck in the back of that chair by mistake. I saw it as an excuse to spend more time with me because she thought I was talented and extra special. She drew dark paint around her eyes, her hair was spiked like she'd just had a fright, and when she spoke her mouth smelt of cold outdoor smoke and Wrigley's Spearmint gum.

Sometimes I'd say something when I wasn't even trying to be funny and she'd laugh and her eyes would go all wet and warm. But at other times I'd say something that I was pretty certain was funny to Patsy, in an especially loud voice, and she mightn't even smile or else she wouldn't be listening; she'd be looking at the horse that Samantha Jennings had drawn, saying how she'd got the legs just right. She'd bend down beside Samantha to have a closer look and put her arm around the back of her chair, and tell her, very close up, everything that was good about her work. And then she'd walk behind me without stopping to look at the clouds that I'd painted, wet watery blues and soft drifting whites.

I made Patsy agree that she often gave me extra atten-tion. She had a small crush on her too but knew she was more my type being a tomboy. When Patsy moved to our school I had someone to be in charge of for the first time. This gave me power; I was the bully of one. I wore my overall with the buttons open, took up spitting for a day, ran down corridors past the simple girl who was scared of everything, with her tight curls, wild eyes and a string of mucus dangling from her nose. The only time she got anyone's attention was when she pulled down her pants and showed her hefty bum to Mr Tetley, the school builder. I imagined her fingers twitching in her pockets, tugging at threads, sweating, flicking. Unlike the simple girl, I had a friend, and I knew more than her. If Patsy stepped out of line I could crush her with my taunt: 'Patsy's half-American' – it always made her cry. Secretly I wanted to be half-American more than anything.

On a day when it was too nice to be inside, Billie decided we should have class in the garden. I climbed up the oak tree in front of the kindergarten school, as high as I could without being scared, and tried to draw my picture from there. Billie came over to see how I was getting along and had to climb up a bit of the tree herself just to look at my sketch. She said there was a great sense of height about it. Then she said how important it was to look at things differently. I hadn't painted the kinder-garten school at all, but my speciality, clouds and sky. I spoiled it all by boasting and exaggerating to Patsy about what Billie had said, not noticing that she was standing under the tree listening. I didn't want to kiss Billie, I didn't know how. But the day became happy when she was close by, when she sat down beside me to say something particular.

I thought I saw Billie twice in the queue for communion – the way she walked, a jacket like hers. Why wasn't she there? I thought everyone in Ireland had to be; I thought it was compulsory. God was bound to notice her missing. Was she not worried about what He might do to punish her? Maybe I'd go to Hell too for having a crush on someone who didn't believe in Him, though wouldn't everyone up at the front be guaranteed a place in Heaven? The people behind us must have been nervous – stuck all the way back in limbo land. Did it matter if I was there but not concentrating? Could He see into my head?

I pictured Billie alone in an empty city. I wondered what it would be like to be the only two people in the world. To drive a Rolls-Royce down Grafton Street, taking anything we wanted – a silver Chopper, black Sasperillas from the Jean Machine, to help ourselves to Skittles and Coke from the mini-bar in a five star hotel. I could show Billie some things she mightn't know about, like the air-raid shelter near Palmerstown Park, and the secret entrance to the Iveagh Gardens. It would be my own small universe, one that I could rule over and arrange, giant-like and in charge, the way I felt when I peered into rock pools in Connemara: forest, mountains, sea, a Clark sandal at each end, a snuffling face of concentration in between. The funny thing was that even if she didn't know it, even if she didn't want to be, Billie was in the Phoenix Park with me and the Pope.

And there had been something else in the air that day that no one had noticed. A bright and shiny tinsel-blue thing, out of place and moving on a different level to the crowd: a tiny flash of lightning above all our greys and browns. It circled me and hovered for a moment between my eyes. I blinked and it darted away and upwards, zigzagging about in mid-air. With my head bent back I traced its erratic journey, diving, twirling, flashing through the sky. Its wings were purple at the edges, like the foil from a Dairy Milk, with light, chocolate-flake-coloured fibres at their centre. Its spiralled body was stiff and shot straight out behind; a miniature hang-glider. I lunged backwards to follow it, pulling at my lips to keep a smile from developing, lest anyone notice that I was, for that moment, happy. My father, having returned to his family now that the chaos of feeding us had finished, turned round and standing up, irritated, he traced its movement too, his Bible opened beneath it like a crazed worshipper. He waited, waited, then 'Got you!' he said, snapping the Bible closed. He opened it again instantly to be satisfied the dragonfly was dead.

I wore my purple sweatshirt under my overall the next Monday at school. I was excited about seeing Billie again, to become even better friends than we were at the weekend. But she wasn't in so we had to have double PE instead. I wanted the day to be over to see if she'd be back the next day. What if she didn't come back at all? And if she really liked me that much why would she miss an opportunity to see me? This was an ominous sign. She was my motivation for going to school even when I was sick. Mrs Buckley made me borrow Sarah O'Brien's spare gym skirt, which was too short and tight for me, because I'd left my tracksuit bottoms at home. She must have forgotten that I didn't wear skirts.

The Big Room echoed like a swimming pool with whistles and screams and the stretched squeak of runners chasing basketballs. My team were doing forward rolls, which I wasn't a bit happy about, as there was a hole in my knickers in a bad place.

When it was my turn, I started in the right position – head up, legs together, arms straight – but at the middle bit, on my back and upside down, I made myself veer off to the side, so no one would notice the hole. Mrs Buckley blew her whistle. 'Do it again!' Again and again I rolled and each time I turned, I could feel the hole grow. The salty feet smell of the rubber and the dizziness of my revolving head were making me sick. And I knew as soon as I stood up that I'd have to roll over again, 'because you're still not doing it right!' The more I rolled the more everyone watched: Mrs Buckley then Jenny Brady then Eimear Kinsella and Joanna Blake. I hated Joanna Blake.

I thumped my Chopper down the steps of the side passageway when I got back from school that afternoon. It was four o'clock, the time of day I hated most. Not proper like morning, cold and new and bright, up early with lots of things to do. Or still and safely locked up and blown out like orange candlelight night. Just flat grey dull old four. A languid cat stretches along a stone wall at a nothing time of day.

I hoped the new fridge had arrived. The one we were getting was the latest model by Bosch with a separate compartment at the front from which you could pour cold water. I imagined what it would feel like to use – the rattle of bottles as I opened it, the heavy clunk as it closed, and the sort of things it would contain. It would be like the one in *The Brady Bunch*, full of Coke and cheese singles and pizzas and hot dogs unpacked from brown paper bags.

I'd forgotten that the boy whose Mum died was staying with us. I don't know why he was there but we were told to be nice to him. She'd gone to get her hair done in Dun Laoghaire and was crossing the road with it freshly styled and set when a bin lorry reversed over her by mistake. I pictured her flat except for her big blow-dried hair, like that squished squirrel I'd seen on our road – its fuzzy tail full of life and sticking up in the air.

He rubbed his nose with his fingers when he saw me – he was leaning against the tool shed in the side passageway, one leg folded behind him. His white shirt was half out of his school trousers, which I thought looked good. And I liked his name, Nat. He was holding something behind his back. When a twist of smoke rose, I felt scared of him because what he was doing was so secret and so wrong. His eyes looked sore from crying or maybe from the smoke and he smelt of oranges and trapped feet.

That evening Nat kissed Pie. I was in bed reading *The Dandy* when it happened; Pie was beside me, indulging in her two main hobbies – God and the Royal family. She was sticking newspaper cuttings of Lady Diana and Prince Charles into her blue photo album illustrated with the Queen's Guards, while singing 'Seek Ye First'.

Nat came in without knocking. I stuck out my tongue, but he didn't say anything back. He went over to Pie and pulled her up by the hair, which sounds strange and sore but it wasn't like that because as he pulled, Pie moved up with her hair. Then he put his mouth on her mouth for at least five seconds and when he stopped, but was still close to her mouth and smiling, he said, 'Will you think about it?' I kicked off my blankets and ran upstairs to the bathroom cabinet. How could Pie have let him do that? I had a good mind to tell Nat that he was wasting his time; Pie was already in love with someone else. I knew for a fact that she had written to *Jim'll Fix It* to fix it for her to go on a date with Prince Andrew.

When I got back in a hurry, her nose looked all swollen and sore like Father Perry's but she wouldn't take the capful of Listerine I proffered. She told me to stop being so mean to Nat, that she didn't mind him kissing her. Then she told me to leave her alone.

'Pie face has her period! Pie face has her period!' I wasn't sure what having a period was but I chanted it all the same, like I always did when we were having a fight. I slammed the bedroom door and went back up to the bathroom; I needed the loo.

I took a copy of the *Phoenix* from the pile of news-papers and magazines on the floor, tore a strip from it and wiped myself. My father had confiscated the toilet roll because he said we were using too much. Under the new house rules it would be utilized only by guests and on special occasions. As the paper flushed away, Charles Haughey's head was smeared in blood. There was some Sudocrem on the side of the bath, which my sister had been using for her spots. I stretched over, pyjamas around knees, and put lots of it down there. It didn't stop the blood, so I folded up the rest of the magazine and lodged it in my knickers. It felt hard and scratchy against my skin, and when I moved it kept slipping out of place.

I wore my new sleeveless blue puffa jacket for our school retreat to Glendalough two days later. My mother said she thought it was 'snazzy and with it' when she bought it from Winstons for me. No one else on the bus was wearing a sleeveless jacket and no one had asked me where I'd bought mine. No one had said anything about it at all. And I hadn't noticed anyone being especially nice to me, which was a definite sign that I should never have nagged Mum into buying it for me. People were friendly to me the day I wore my purple sweatshirt; that's why I wore it for a whole week. I took my puffa jacket off and sat on it. Just thinking about Mum was making me homesick.

The bleeding still hadn't stopped. The ointment hadn't healed the cut and the newspapers were digging into me, but the trick was to stay absolutely still. Nothing would happen so long as I stayed still.

Then the bus driver said what about a song. And because people knew about my lovely voice, everyone begged us to do 'Ebony and Ivory'. I took the high bits for this particular number, which surprised people because of me being like a boy and chubby; Patsy did the deep, low parts, even though she was bony with a nose like a shark's fin.

But as I reached the chorus, the blood began to seep. It soaked through the newspaper, through my trousers, and onto my puffa jacket. I prayed that it hadn't reached the seat. Then I couldn't stop it, even after our song was over, even when I was still, hot swollen drips issued out of me. I prayed to God that no one else could smell its burnt heat.

A woman in a white coat called Nurse Kelly opened all the windows in our classroom several weeks later, when she came in to give us an extra-curricular class on menstruation and personal hygiene. She seemed to take relish in mortifying us as she talked about private parts. Standing too close to me one afternoon – all hushed and bosomy and intimate – she told me that I was becoming a young woman.

Nurse Kelly seemed to think it was a positive development, a wonderful, womanly bosomy thing. But the last thing I wanted was to become a woman; I wasn't even happy about being a girl. My plan was to stay a boy, to join the army – not to get killed or do any fighting or anything risky like that – but to run through obstacle courses, mud spattering my face, to crawl beneath nets and swing on tyres and climb over huge wooden frames, to sing 'When The Saints Go Marching In'. To tumble down sand dunes wearing just my jeans, with the band of my white underpants peeping out against the sallow skin of my back. To catch fish for my lunch like Huckleberry Finn in rolled-up dungarees and bare feet treading dusty ground, dangling in still green ponds under tree houses and tadpoles and torches and tents and cuts on my knees and a long scar through the brow of my good eye.

Mum kept leaving salmon-pink packages on my bed. They made me cross – I hated them. I hid them in Pie's underwear drawer, and stuffed my bloody knickers down the back of the dressing table. Mrs McCabe pulled them back out every Tuesday when she cleaned and threw them in the bin. She also by accident threw out my Memory Box with the decanter label I'd made into a dog tag and my *Late Late Show* ticket, which Gay Byrne had personally signed.

While not tidying my room on a drizzly Saturday afternoon I found in my bedroom cupboard, amongst the usual leftovers from sales of work (pin cushions, lavender soaps, woven hanging baskets) a copy of *The Thorn Birds*. I skipped vast sections of landscape description and dialogue to the bits of the book about periods and sex and men which I read and re-read, shoving it down the side of my bed whenever I heard footfalls on the stairs.

Mrs McCabe told Mum about my underwear, but it didn't change anything between us; we still couldn't mention the 'P' word. I'd seen an unwrapped sanitary towel twice in real life, once on each of Tracy Kenny's knees when she'd used them as shin pads for hockey; once on Joanna Blake's little brother's face: his Mum had looped the ends round his ears, and put the padded bit under his cut chin, but I couldn't even take one out of its packaging and I dreaded that panty pad advert with the ice skater on TV. I talked over it immediately whenever it came on; Mum would untuck her slippered feet from where she'd been sitting on them and say she had better just check my father's liver under the grill.

4

Sea change

I waited for the next wave to come, arms wide, treading the blue green, basking in the brief warmth of the spot where I'd just weed. Surging forwards when it came, gulping its salt taste, I let it carry me towards the shore. I was on my knees, struggling to stand, when it dragged me back out and under, shingle peppering my belly.

I thrashed my arms and legs about in the silence underwater, like a moving image on a mute TV. Battling upwards, a kaleidoscope of memories from my short life flashed before me, which was disconcerting in two ways: because nothing had really happened yet and because I'd heard that this was what people experience before they drown.

I surfaced and shouted – my voice as tiny and useless as someone fallen overboard from a disappearing cruise ship – only for another wave to come crashing down, plunging me under again. I was drowning and no one had noticed. It was when I'd finally re-emerged in a lull, re-orientated myself, and was swimming safely to shore, that I heard my mother's voice. It sounded distant and in the wrong direction and increasingly anxious. I was heading, not for land, but for the horizon; I was dog paddling haplessly towards America.

This was Ollie's moment. He stood by the water's edge trying to spot me, one lanky arm akimbo, the other bent over his eyes. The sun in his face was a stage light. He moved through the surf, dolphin-style, and swam out to me. Hyperventilating and spluttering but delighted to be alive I let him hold me under the chin and guide me back to shore. Aware of the audience of adults on the beach, he played the cool cut, no bother hero, me the dramatically weak and frail victim.

In safely shallow water we separated; Ollie fought forwards in manly strides through the swell, his taut chest expanding and deflating with exertion. I was lifted by another wave, but got onto my feet, yanking my togs into place and making gapped curtains of my sodden, pudding-bowl hair, before it had a chance to pull me out again. Oscar's head bobbed in the swollen grey sea behind us, as he tugged Patsy on their lilo ashore – a flotation device that our father had forbidden us from using, for fear that it might carry us away.

It was the last day of our summer holidays and a swim had only been agreed to once all our bunk beds had been stripped, the car packed up, and the bucket under the electricity meter in the hall emptied of its seaweed and sand.

We shook sand from towels on the beach; my father closed his book at the first spots of rain and began to disassemble the windbreaker. He moved in fits and starts as he set about folding it up, methodical and meticulous at first, but the wind corrupted each attempt he made and he struggled, cartoon-like, impatient to get the job done, venting his frustration on the awkward origami of wood and canvas that was delaying him.

We dripped around the adults, shivering for attention while they allocated towels and dry clothes, then raced each other over to the sand dunes, as far away as we could to disassociate ourselves from them and my brothers and sister, whose company I resented and didn't require when I was with my friends. Luckily the Frog was having one of his nosebleeds so he couldn't follow us. Patsy moved along the water's edge, showing off that she could run through the sea without splashing, unaware until that holiday that this was a wholly desirable talent, one that I envied and with my stubby solid legs would never possess.

In the shelter of a dune we peeled off our togs, struggling to roll them down while keeping our towels in place – mine and Patsy's secured under our arms,

Oscar's around his waist. It was my idea to get under the picnic rug together. The modesty of the moment before was forgotten: a curiosity took over. A curiosity for what, we weren't sure: a small act of rebellion before the enforced order of school.

Free and naked we wriggled about trying to cover extremities, our bodies goose-pimpled, taut. Patsy's dripping hair slapped in my face as she turned, her angular limbs digging into me; Oscar struggled between us to get warm, brushing his cool bottom against my leg, toenails scratching, tickling each other unintentionally, sand everywhere.

And for a moment we were still; we studied each other through the light penetrating the petrol-blue check, our breath warming the air inside the rug, exhilaration making our hearts thump. We all wanted to be there but none of us knew why or what we should do next.

I noticed the smell. We smelt different: heavier, fleshy, sour. Patsy's raised arms were a secret exposed: tufts of sprouting hair. Oscar looked at my breasts – fresh buns. Although he was three years younger than me I had often considered marrying him: his deep-set almond eyes, the long dry lashes shielding them, the boyishness of his grazed knees and chewed nails, the downy hair between his shoulder blades, his clean, suntanned feet in sandals. His chest was sallow and smooth; I followed it from nipples to belly button and beyond. It led to something unexpected: I saw between his legs with a fright something I should not have seen, a fleshy knot, like a fledgling in its nest.

My father's voice coming towards us panicked us to get dressed. Frightened, ashamed, with sand in our socks and bum cheeks, we tugged at our knickers, still damp and not properly in place. Oscar cursed, trying out the sound of a newly learnt swear word. Only Oscar and Patsy's mother noticed anything different about us and asked why Oscar's tank top was inside out.

I lay on the floor beneath the back seat of the car on our journey home to Dublin that night. I loved the heat of the engine and the motion and seeing the world from upside down, the gentle indicator tick, the passing telegraph poles, the voices above me, Radio Four, being womb-like, curled up, cocooned. My parents allowed it but without saying anything I knew that it was the last time I would be lying down there. Time was ticking biologically, altering life and thoughts, readying for something new. I was thinking more about being a proper girl; I tried to picture my legs in a skirt. I licked the leather seat.

Back in Dublin, the subject of my eyesight was raised for the first time, and an appointment was made with Doctor McNally, a squat, bald man who walked briskly – despite one leg being several inches shorter than the other – and talked briskly, and answered his own questions: 'Why? I'll tell you why.' He looked old the way a newborn chicken looks, wispy-haired, shrivel-skinned, angular. So that's what a bird-like man was. The sort of bird-like man I'd been told to be at Billie Barry Stage

School, but I hadn't understood what bird-like meant which perplexed me so much that I forgot every line of my soliloquy. I sat on stage, on a park bench in a belted mackintosh, saying nothing at all, while my mother, in the front row with her box of Quality Street, searched for the adjectives she'd have to come up with to describe my performance when she would eventually collect me backstage.

My eye report was as disappointing as my school reports: a minus four in the left and a minus five plus astigmatism in the right. By the time Doctor McNally diagnosed it, it was too late to do anything about my lazy eye – too late for a patch, too late to force my weak eye to work. And that wasn't the only problem. While everyone else in the world had spherical eyes, mine were oval, like a football that someone had sat on.

'She has the same weak eyes as her father,' Doctor McNally said to Mum, as he wrote my prescription, then bent to tell me that I could choose any pair I wanted from the selection along the wall, as though this was something I would savour – my first pair of glasses – as though they were not glasses at all but jars of chocolate cushions and lemon drops.

While I tried on various models of sugar-pink and watery-blue frames, I overheard Doctor McNally continue, more softly: 'It's a shame the lazy eye wasn't spotted earlier. It really is vital for children to develop equal vision in both eyes for them to function normally. Why? Because sharpness of sight and two-eyed binocular vision are essential to succeed in life: in school, sports, or any other activity that requires good vision, good hand-eye coordination and strong depth perception.' I could hear Mum tutting about my bad luck in response, mumbling and making excuses for not having noticed it earlier, hurrying the doctor along with lots of yes yes yeses and away from further bad news. 'What happens when a lazy eye is left untreated?' The doctor went on, 'When children with untreated amblyopia become adults, their choice of career may be limited and, if they are unlucky enough to lose vision in their one good eye, they could be visually impaired or legally blind for life.'

I lay in bed that night and tried to identify familiar objects in the dark. Why hadn't anyone noticed that there was something wrong with me before? Why hadn't I been given a patch to wear? Would I, as my condition worsened, be packed off to a blind school down in the countryside, some ancient institution run by faceless old nuns in habits, like the ones in the *Armchair Thrillers*, where children in grey shorts behave unpredictably, slur when they speak, always too loudly, pink contraptions stuck to their heads and dangling from their chests, wailing when pulled from the cars of their parents by the firm cold hand of the abbess? Would my lazy eye close and twitch like our Maths teacher's did when she tried to multiply numbers in her head? Could it eventually cloud over and give up? What if the other one went too? What if I went blind? I buried my face in the bedclothes, and wallowing in self-pity, chest tightening, throat constricting at the tragedy of my fate, I considered one final, frightening question: could blind people still dream?

With the new school year came new freedom and permission to explore beyond the gates at lunchtime. We freewheeled down the dual carriageway towards Donnybrook, bellowing at each other through the wind, Patsy on her brand-new Triumph Twenty, me on Mum's foldable Moulton Stowaway and always slightly ahead, despite Patsy's aerodynamically superior face. My Chopper had a flat tyre; I let the Frog use it more these days.

Patsy and I were getting along great, provided I didn't mention anything whatsoever about the inter-school production of *Grease* we had auditioned for the previous week. Patsy had sung 'Happy Birthday'; I chose 'Penny Lane' and had to begin it twice as I started off too high on my first attempt, leaving my voice with nowhere to travel by the time I'd reached the chorus.

They said that they'd get back to us, which sounded promising and then not promising and then promising again.

I was over at Patsy's a few evenings later, when she received a call from one of the judges, a Mrs Meredith, informing her that she had been successful and offering her the part of one of the cheerleaders. Spurred on I phoned home, heart pounding, to see if there had been a call for me, Patsy and her mother standing by, ears cocked. There had been – I was in! Patsy clapped; her mother slapped my shoulder. But there was more: I had been asked to re-audition for a solo. This changed everything.

We sat on Patsy's bed as she swung between sobbing, flinging things and sighing. These sighing attacks – deep, chest-heaving inhalations – were always triggered by something going right for me. I tried to reassure her, suggested that we call Mrs Meredith back to check if there'd been a mistake. Inside I was bubbling with excitement, full of nervous energy at my impending stardom. I felt talented for the first time in my life. Even my hands looked different as I tickled Patsy's Jack Russell, Arthur, on the belly – more American, actor-like, slim.

I plumped for my usual at Abrakebabra – cheesy chips and a large Coke. Patsy deliberated over spicy wedges and chilli fries. We sat on high stools and waited for Sam, Floor Manager of Abrakebabra, Donnybrook, to join us on his tea break. I loved that he put on an Australian accent when he spoke to us, even though he was from Athlone. 'G'day, matey!' he'd say. I loved that his right eye closed over when he laughed.

My favourite thing about him was the way he wore a white T-shirt under his brown Abrakebabra top – along with his Floor Manager badge, it made him look like the blond one from *Starsky and Hutch*. The hair on his forearms was slick black and bristled up over his digital watch, and the ones crawling over the top of his T-shirt were just about the hunkiest things I'd ever seen. But the hair on his head was bouncy and fair and I couldn't work out whether he would be fair or dark in his private parts. The only other thing that worried me about him was his mouth. It seemed unusually small, even when he smiled, his teeth huddled up like fat chiclets inside.

We answered his questions in unison – we competed for attention of any sort, particularly male, which made us hyper as aside from our brothers who didn't really count we had almost no experience of how to behave around them – and showed off, telling our best stories with accompanying gestures: stamping feet, snorting Coke, ribs clutched in mock hilarity.

Back we went to visit Sam after school the next afternoon, back to visit our first proper male friend. Light faded as we swung on our stools being hilarious, but he still wouldn't take a tea break. We had read about how important it was not to make the first move – not that we knew quite how a move was made – so at eight o'clock that evening we got up and casually left. I peeped back at him on our way out to see if he might be watching, but he was busy fiddling some wax from his right ear with the rubber bit of a pencil and didn't even look up.

As we pushed our bikes through Donnybrook, time lost to us, I explained to Patsy that that's just how men were, using my father as a point in case. Sometimes he'd eat with us, like when Mum was in hospital having her varicose vein pulled out, on other days he'd carry his lunch on a tray into his study. Neither of us noticed Patsy's mother pulling up in her car.

I stood well out of the way, wincing with each whack

Patsy was delivered, on the backs of her legs, her bum, wherever her mother could reach. Did she have any idea how late it was? She had been about to call the police. Where the bloody hell had we been? Little did I know that I was next in line – I was pulled from my bike and walloped hard on the behind.

I found simply speaking to Patsy's mother excruciating, so the intimate humiliation of being spanked by her in public almost winded me with shock and indignation. Accustomed to roaring abuse and threats at my own parents, I was far too polite to answer back to those of a friend, too frightened to defend myself in any way. I silently endured my beating and swore private revenge. Just who did she think she was, assaulting me, a young woman of fourteen and three quarters?

When I told Mum of this injustice, she defended Patsy's mother – whatever it took to keep the peace – and excused my beating by saying that she had got an awful fright, that it just wasn't safe to be roaming around at that hour, particularly since the murder of that nurse in the Phoenix Park.

I hated when people behaved unpredictably – it didn't only startle me, I found it embarrassing. I remembered yearning for my parents to come home from Italy following a week under the supervision of Mrs Grimshaw. 'Yoo-hoo!' she'd call out when she collected us from school, waving with her fingers, in a mossy cardigan, lace-up shoes, grey hair clipped at the sides, a wicker basket lodged beneath her bosom. I imagined the racket all those yoo-hoos would make in the village from which she came, all those Protestant old ladies yoo-hoo-ing at each other across the High Street, on their way to the Sunday market or to the Singing Kettle cake shop for tea.

Unidentifiable things lurked in our homemade meals – Irish Stew surprise, apple snow avec hair. Mrs Grimshaw would join us, flumping onto the kitchen bench in her kilt, to ensure that we ate every last bit and washed it all down with diluted Pripsen powder (she suspected we had worms).

It was during a power cut one evening that I got sweet, unintentional revenge. Everyone was searching for a torch and I was sure I'd seen one in the spare room where Mrs Grimshaw was staying. I scampered back downstairs proudly holding the black, torch-like barrel in my hand, pushed the button on its side, but, instead of the expected redeeming light, it began to wriggle and vibrate. Mrs Grimshaw snatched it from me, muted the drilling sound and stuffed it into her handbag. Ollie was giggling so much behind her that he had to hold his hand between his trouser legs to stop from wetting himself. I wasn't sure just what had happened, but I was pretty certain I shouldn't ask.

The curtains were parted constantly on the evening my parents were due home, our four reflections appearing in the drawing-room window as it got dark. 'Here they are!' I'd shout every so often, mistaking another car for theirs. I couldn't recall ever having been so excited about seeing them, I even emptied the dishwasher in prospect of their arrival, giving myself a lump in my throat so moved was I by my own heroic and unseen gesture.

When they finally came through the front door, my father in the outfit he always wore on holidays – a peppermint blue shirt, cream trousers and a brown belt, just like an Italian – I leapt from the sofa without thinking, in a moment of pure excitement and relief and flung myself at him, arms clasping his neck, legs gripping around his waist. I mistimed my take off and had misjudged my position on the chair and his position in the hall and had to cling onto his shirt to stop myself from falling.

I felt something give. He threw me back onto the sofa. I bounced and laughed, thinking it was a game, but then came his hand hard on my face and again and again on my legs. I'd torn his favourite peppermint blue shirt.

I was back to the old me on the day of the solo auditions for *Grease* and too terrified to go in. Patsy had accompanied me for moral support. We took turns peeping through the window at a scene almost identical to the one we'd faced a fortnight before: a line of tables where the judges were sitting, fidgeting auditionees along the wall, numbers pinned to their chests, deep breaths, stage school American accents, tap dancing to jaunty piano keys.

We sat on the embankment outside the school hall, deliberating. 'You *poor* thing,' Patsy said, with one of her sighs, 'I'd *hate* to be you. There's no way in the whole world I could go in there.' Her voice didn't sound normal, it was at least an octave too high and she was speaking inordinately fast. I yanked grass from the earth in clumps, coming around to her point of view. It didn't occur to either of us that we had both managed it quite happily a fortnight earlier. Patsy then suggested, and I reluctantly agreed, that it would be better to forget all about the audition, either way by that stage it was probably too late to go in.

'Why don't we have a game of tennis?' Patsy brightened, jumping up, brushing grass off her bum. 'Get some Loop the Loops?' It was all I needed, an excuse to opt out. We picked up our bikes and rode out the school gates, both of us hugely relieved. I knew I was being subtly led away.

Tennis was a hobby we had recently taken up, and one that I had developed quite a flair for, particularly since enlisting Patsy as my ball machine. I grunted and walloped returns at her down at our local club, which she ducked to avoid, racket shielding her face, before running off to retrieve them from where they'd crashed beyond her, against the back fence. We were quite happy with this arrangement as our real motivation for being there was to watch, and perhaps one happy day actually talk to, the club's most talented young males mopping sweat from their foreheads on biceps, allowing us tantalizing glimpses of drenched and glistening underarm hair, their tanned, muscular thighs in irresistibly strained tennis shorts.

At first rehearsal the following week, Mrs Meredith singled me out and asked why I hadn't appeared. I mumbled something about a sore throat and was awarded, to giggles and nudges around me, the undesirable consolation prize of understudy to Danny, the male lead.

One school afternoon when we just so happened to be wheeling our bikes past the windows of Abrakebabra, all nonchalant and not looking in, Sam drummed on the pane and shouted, 'G'day!' He was slicing slivers of meat from the twirling kebab spit and unmistakably winked at me. He was also down at the far end of the counter, near the till, pouring Coke from the drinks dispenser while re-tucking his shirt into the back of his synthetic trousers, then tugging to free something caught near his zip.

Though they were born identical twins, there were six differences between Sam and Shane. They listed these as we sat between them amazed: a furry mole under Shane's left ear, a birthmark on the back of Sam's knee, some others that I can't recall, but the seventh one was that Sam wanted to go with me.

He popped the question one afternoon, while Patsy was on holidays in America and I was in Abrakebabra on my own. I wasn't a bit happy about sitting there for no reason, especially as I didn't have any pocket money left to buy a drink, and was about to leave when Sam took his hat off and sat down to join me, smelling of Old Spice and shish kebab. He asked if I was free on

Saturday night to 'do something'. My ears were hot; I felt a heavy sensation in my bladder. I was being asked out, I could not wait to tell Patsy. I had no idea what 'doing something' might entail, but it seemed like the most exciting thing in the world.

We met after his football match that Saturday night. He caught me as I jumped from the spiked fence into Harold's Cross Park. It was his turn to wash the team's kit, he said, as he spread two sweaty red and white shirts beside each other on the grass for us to lie on.

I was wearing a green woollen polo-neck jumper I'd transformed with the little Lacoste alligator I'd cut out of Ollie's tennis shorts. I'd sewn it on just above my left boob and I'd borrowed one of Pie's bras for the occasion, which made me feel womanly and ashamed and peculiar and erotic and tingly downstairs, all at the same time.

My beige ski pants had looked OK when I'd put them on, and contrasted well with the green of the alligator, but the knees had gone baggy, even with the elasticated stirrup bits under my feet pulling them straight.

Sam took a can of Carlsberg from a plastic Spar bag, and passed me a bottle of Babycham. I loved the way his leather jacket squeaked as he put his arm around my shoulders, but I was scared he might try to kiss me. I was still worried about the whole mouth thing, about them being different sizes and not fitting each other with his being so tiny and full of teeth, and mine being roomy as anything. I had no idea how I was supposed to breathe and kiss at the same time, where I was meant to keep my tongue, whether I should approach him head on, or from the side at a tilt, and if so, which side should I tilt to? Eyes open or closed? And what about my hands?

I made Sam laugh. 'Come here, bright eyes,' he said as he moved over to me, opened his mouth over mine and poked his tongue in out in out in out the way a chameleon might. He kept telling me to lick my lips, that they were too dry, but once I'd got the hang of it, I couldn't stop. Not just his mouth, I kissed his nose and his ears and both his eyelids. He had to break a line of saliva between us a few times, which I didn't tell Patsy about, and as we kissed I could feel his thingamajig against my leg which I didn't tell Patsy about either. I didn't dare look down or put my hand anywhere near it but I could feel it pointing in my direction, which I was pretty sure must mean that he liked me. And when I said something silly, I couldn't feel it anymore and I knew that it must have turned the other way.

In the dark of my bedroom I taught Patsy how to kiss. We'd experimented since that day on the beach; we'd pulled down our knickers to compare fluffy bits and we'd done some exploring with a toothbrush in the derelict house on Rat's Lane. I'd stolen a condom from Ollie's wallet with the map of Thailand on it and put it over the broken arm of my rag doll, though I wasn't sure what to do next.

Patsy hadn't been a bit happy about Sam asking me out and would have preferred not to discuss the kiss at all had I not been in possession of such new and invaluable knowledge. She had just come back from America with two things I didn't have: a FAME sweatshirt in pink and a New York accent. I felt justified in boasting. I wondered was it visible, the change that had happened to me? I felt it must have been.

I told her to bend her tongue back as far as it could go, as near to her tonsils as she could reach, then to wriggle it around, out and in, up down, back and forth. That's what a kiss felt like.

We lay eyes wide in the dark, with our tongues down our throats, trying it out for a while. Then we scared each other like we always did by talking about Rumpelstiltskin racing through my room in a rage, in his eerie old striped tights and stamping his foot through the floor. We did a few Billy Joel numbers – Patsy said she didn't mind if I rocked – followed by 'He is Lord', I don't know how many times, but we didn't stop until we'd got the harmony just right.

5

Scrabble

The keys to Sea Spray had not been hidden behind the boulder daubed with turquoise as agreed. Back into the car and back down the boreen we went, jolted and re-arranged, petrol sloshing in the reserve tank, snarling up the hill by the thatched cottage, lurching close enough to momentarily glimpse through its window a model ship and sea urchins tangled artistically in nets. We paused on the slope, engine trembling; Mum got out to unlock the gate, her hair and coat flapping about in the gale, then over and down, stomachs heaving, Mum back in with a rush of peaty air, and on into unseen holes and jutting rocks, by fields of scattering sheep and a man walking his bicycle, who pinned himself unsmiling against a stone wall to let us pass. My father cursed at the damage he was doing to the tyres, our ancient Fiat careering wildly down the lane. The swell and drag motion of the swollen grey sea just beyond.

We were ordered, all of us, including my mother, to remain in the car, which was now on a promontory opposite the village high street. Father went in search of the owner of the cottage whom we called Mr Fisher-

King – a local fisherman who also owned King's shoe shop, King's greengrocers and King's funeral home.

Stale and woozy after an interminable drive from Dublin, the vegetable soup slurped in a harbour bar an hour earlier still heavy in our stomachs, we chatted and complained lazily over the fuzz of Radio One, its volume always just below audible, the whine of the windscreen wipers taunting us through unremitting rain.

I rolled my window down, allowing a visible cloud of flatulence to blend with the influx of damp salty air and diesel from marooned boats. The scrubland below us sloped down to a pot-holed tennis court, whose ragged net whipped about in the breeze like a misshapen apron, spilling onto a flat stretch of compact sand. Horizontal sheets of rain beat the dun-coloured low tide, and herring gulls screeched, hungry for sprats. The old schoolhouse was still there, the sea-worn swings and slide of earlier summers, where the local children threw baby crabs at our legs and smelt of fireplaces and made a scattering sound on concrete as they ran in their lace-up shoes. 'What are ya gawkin at?' they'd yell in their alien, high-pitched brogues. We knew innately that we did not like them, though even they would have been a welcome sight that day – it was only early August, yet it felt like a seaside town out of season: the bunting that hung across the main street advertising a long dismantled funfair, the rubber rings, flippers and snorkels bunched and tied with twine to the awnings above the corner shop spattered with raindrops, the rusting lobster pots.

That family holiday, which would turn out to be our last, had been ill fated from the start. Aside from the bleak weather, my mother was having problems with her teeth, putting her hand up over her mouth each time she spoke, making us worry at mealtimes and around strangers that the whole lot were going to come out. Pie was inconsolable following Buckingham Palace's announcement of the engagement of Prince Andrew. She was off her food and still in her pyjamas and royal wedding T-shirt at lunchtime, scribbling odes to Andrew and sifting through her album of press photographs and newspaper articles about him. When she could be coaxed outdoors she traced huge love hearts with his and her initials in the sand. I hadn't wanted to be there either – there was a party in Dublin I was missing (that I hadn't been invited to it seemed beside the point). Only Ollie had been considered old and trustworthy enough to be allowed to remain at home alone.

The inclement weather kept us housebound and in each other's company for tortuously dragged out and miss-spelt games of Scrabble. Painstakingly erected card houses were toppled by boxes of groceries to be unpacked – cereal, table salt and tomato ketchup. The black and white portable television in the corner could only offer green reception on RTÉ One and Two, which we glared at from a seventies-style poo brown and blood orange-striped sofa – the sort you see ignited in television adverts for fire safety.

Between squally showers we were ushered out for those two dreaded words – 'brisk walks' – on which I hung back to disassociate myself from my parents: my father with his old-fashioned tweed jacket and bald head, my mother's tapered checked trousers and bunched socks in shoes. This arrangement suited us – my father educated the Frog on local history while Mum talked to Pie about what they might make everyone for lunch, trying to encourage an interest in food.

An under-sixteens' tennis tournament was the only thing that could resurrect that holiday. Mrs Fisher-King – a long, dour, string of a woman with clipped, side-parted, little girl's hair, pointed glasses and a white buttoned-up coat with a pocket for her pen – told my mother about it as she totted her bill up by hand, in a shop that belonged to the past, with its bell over the door and its weighing scales for apple drops in plastic jars and the sun-bleached boxes of washing powder on half-empty shelves. The tournament was a twenty-mile drive from the village we were staying in, but it was agreed to, to give everyone else a bit of relief from my oppressive gloom.

Mum and I searched for my name in the draw; as with all the unseeded players, I had been put up against the number one, Holly or Heather, something blonde and horsey, a traditional way of filtering out the weak, so the real competition could begin. Remarkably, Heather or Holly had to pull out, and I was given a walkover to the second round. This was already the furthest I had ever progressed in a tennis tournament.

I'd been limbering up – stretching, jogging on the spot, doing squats, comparing the tautness of the strings on my rackets (I collected all the ones in the house to trick people into thinking I was sponsored) – when Regina Canning, my second-round opponent, appeared on court. With a face as concave and apologetic as a crescent moon, sweeping into a chest sunken like it had been punched, Regina pulled the cover off her wooden racket, which was warped and missing a string. She fished around a plastic bag containing a hairbrush and a browning banana, for three balding tennis balls. I was staring victory in the face.

With a few final stretches and a slug of Lucozade, I positioned myself on the baseline, racket twirling, bottom wiggling, and waited for my opponent to serve.

Ball after ugly ball came at me: hit high, off the wood, flukes of every sort. Occasionally one would land pleasingly plump and low. Thumping forward to attack it, I saw the perfect shot in my head. I could hear the fat puck it would make as it came in contact with the centre of the strings, the precise position of its landing on the other side of the net. I saw it all clearly in my head, the clean luminosity of a brand-new missile charging through the air, my tanned hand, the white Swatch watch around my wrist. I even smelt it – the heady rubber from a freshly opened can.

My glasses steamed with my breath, I charged towards the net, tongue to the side in concentration, grunted and walloped every ball back too hard, too high, too long, over the fence, argued calls, cursed with frustration, told a few fibs. When it started to drizzle in the second set, Regina pulled up an umbrella and flailed around the court with it held in one hand. We were level at four games each in the third when the tournament organiser suggested that we call it a night and finish the match the following day.

I demanded praise for my performance and faith in my ability to win as we wound over the mountain top that evening on our way back to the holiday house. 'Yes, it was a great match, very tight, yes. Yes, you're a great girl,' my mother assured me as we passed ferns and waterfalls and dripping mossy grottos of the Virgin Mary gazing heavenward, faded blue hydrangea bushes and stone statues of eagles in driveways and sparrows riding fuchsia bushes in the breeze.

Back at Sea Spray we were met by an idyllic family scene: fire alight, the Frog reading a book in his favourite position – standing up and leaning against the top of an armchair, always about to be doing something more constructive – Pie cooking omelettes for everyone in the kitchen, my father under the soft light of a standard lamp in the corner with his portable typewriter and Jameson's, catching up on some work.

I related my struggle and progression and added that I was going back to seal my victory at ten o'clock the following morning. I visualized mid-action shots of me in the local papers, kissing the tournament trophy with photographers calling my name, a previously unheard of but exciting and gifted new player from the city.

'Absolutely not,' my father said without looking up from his typewriter. 'Under no circumstances whatsoever.'

'Dad, I wasn't talking to you.'

'You can't expect your poor mother to drive another twenty miles for some silly tennis game, especially with that abscess on her tooth. And who do you expect to pay for the petrol?'

To my father any sort of sport was a nonsensical waste of time. He viewed his own body as nothing more than a vehicle for carrying his head around. He, like the rest of us, hadn't considered the possibility of my progressing beyond the first round. With my track record it was assumed that it would be one match only and swiftly forgotten about.

'But she doesn't mind. Sure you don't Mum? Mum didn't you say it was a lovely drive?'

'Ah, for pity's sake, Bunty. Don't make me argue with you.'

I let Mum take over and listened to them argue it out. Whimpering with the certainty that I wouldn't be returning to the tournament I climbed into my bunk bed and lay under a crinoline eiderdown on its damp mattress, foam coming through a tear in the candy-striped sheet. Damp spread above me too, like a wet-bed stain across the ceiling. Mum would lose; she was useless at arguing. It was something she never wanted to be involved in; confrontation always silenced her.

Truthfully, I didn't especially want to finish the match – I was terrified of losing it and this way there could be no real loser. It was the principle I was arguing, the principle of not being supported when I was trying to do something right. I wasn't going to let my father away with this.

He had opened the fridge door and was holding a bottle of milk when I marched into the kitchen, cruising for a fight.

He peeled off its cap and sniffed at it to check its freshness – one thicket-thick brow arched. A jagged bit of toilet paper clung to the sandpaper-like skin beneath his chin. He must have cut himself shaving.

The kitchen seemed to have contracted since the summer before. Always dark and tightly packed as a ship's cabin, it was now oppressive and closing in: panel-effect beauty board pressed us together from the sides, a knotty pine ceiling weighed down on us from above, the brown and red leaf patterned cushions on the bench seats, the care-home lino floor, worn to beige by the cooker and around the kitchen door. The air was thick with oil from the congealing frying pan in the sink. I felt unable to breathe.

I began arguing my case. He was searching the cupboard for an unchipped glass. Did he have to make so much noise while I was talking? Was he deliberately trying to drown me out like Mum did when I was saying something she didn't want to hear? I waited till he was upright to continue.

He held the glass he'd chosen – a tumbler decorated with watermelons – up to the light. Deciding that it wasn't sufficiently clean, he ran it under the tap. The maroon-coloured alcove behind it was home to too many things: sun-faded John Hinde postcards; seashells and pebbles, glistening and interesting when wet; snow-storms with leprechauns; single rubber gloves; crumbling Brillo pads.

'Hopefully I'll win tomorrow and then ...' I stopped that line of argument when I could see it was leading me down the wrong direction.

'There's no such word as "hopefully",' he said wearily, as he always did when any of us used that word. We never understood why.

'OK, but if I win tomorrow, hopefully ...'

There was a pause. He turned and stared at me.

'OK, Dad! But don't you call me Bunty anymore! I'm not Bunty, I'm Lucy. Lucy Bastonme. Lucy Bastonme. Bunty is a fat baby's name.'

His combination of shirt and swimming trunks looked silly. His paunch bulged under the straining buttons of his shirt, disproportionate to his bony legs. The dangling bit of toilet paper was annoying me too, and that he'd had a drink. Whiskey usually mellowed him, made him say my eyes were china blue. I'd got him too early. I seemed to be sobering him up.

I boasted blatantly then, the way you can to your parents. About the comeback I'd made, about how even with a blister on my hand, I'd carried on. He was sitting at the kitchen table and was about to start on a disgusting-looking snack of Bovril on cream crackers. I pulled that face Mum hated when she was trying to enjoy her breakfast of porridge and prunes. He didn't notice. He had propped a copy of *The Irish Times* against the cracker packet so that he could read it while keeping his hands free to eat and drink. He was trying to concentrate on an article.

'Dad,' I whined, throat tightening. 'Why aren't you listening?'

I was standing beside the fridge feeling like an irritant – stuttery, flush-faced, an over-hot lump of menstrual angst – knowing that he was willing me to leave the room but thinking of ways I could get his attention, distract him from his reading, hurt him. I knew he was holding back, still controlling himself, I knew that inside there was a lot more. I pushed him, frightened but full of hot rage. I wanted to make him upset, to make him take me seriously.

And then it came, the crash of fist on table. The knife slid from his plate with a jangle. The lampshade – junkshop frosted glass – rocked, exposing its bulb and leaving a little yellow ball of light floating across my eyes. It drifted across my father's face, onto his plate, along the bridge of his nose. He went for the attack.

Why couldn't I devote some energy into my schoolwork instead of fooling and foostering around like an eejit? When would I ever grow up? Why was I throwing my life away? And did I realize that while I'd been messing and dossing, Alison Hampton next door had come runner up in the Young Scientist of the Year competition.

He was the wrong shape to carry such rage. I was frightened that his body wouldn't be able to take much more pressure. Tiny red corpuscles were charging about the edges of his snake eyes like warnings, the vein on his neck was wildly pulsating.

I may have been fooling and foostering but at least I wasn't drinking my life away, I hurled at him, trembling, my hand on the door handle, ready to make my escape.

We flung all sorts of words at each other then. I tutted and snorted and shouted and swore. Why couldn't he be proud of me? Why did he never listen to me? What was wrong with the way I spoke? I would stand whatever way I wanted. It was my life. I could do as I pleased. Nothing was coming out right; everything was faltering, knee-jerk.

I told him how much I hated him. The toilet paper under his chin had fallen off to reveal a raw, sore-looking cut on the apex of his Adam's apple. I was crying now, headachey, hoarse-throated, teeth vibrating. I was crying because I was hurting him, but I wanted to hurt him more.

The only weapons I had left were tears and a door to slam. We all whacked doors at him; the poor old kitchen door, the anger we couldn't express, the stubbornness of a man we couldn't wear down, the eloquence we had no hope of competing with.

He took a bite out of a cracker, his ears foetal pink with heat. The hand that held the cracker was shaking. Why do upset people look so vulnerable when they eat?

He eyed me as though the very sight of me was objectionable – as though he didn't know where to begin to describe the huge disappointment I had been. Putting his cracker down, he removed his glasses, rubbed the top of his nose between his thumb and first finger and hid his face in his hands. His evening was ruined, his blood pressure was up, he was another day closer to death. A tired small voice in his hands told me to leave him alone.

Lunging at the door, I belted it shut.

'Fuck off!'

6

Ich wurde mindet nicht if du waren virtlich dick

My father used to say that it would take all his influence to get me a job working behind the till at Quinnsworth. This has always looked like a tricky sort of job to me, and I privately suspected, as I rocked in bed on a sunny Saturday afternoon, lurching my dizzy head from pillow to wall and howling along with Madonna, that not even his sway would be sufficient to keep me employed in that particular job.

He modified this to packing bags at the same supermarket when he read my fifth-year school report. It caused him to roll the 'r' in rotten – something I'd never heard him do before. That I'd never heard him do it before suggested that I was in deeper trouble than ever before and that I should probably make a run for it.

These and similar predictions were habitually addressed to my bedroom door. Me on one side, my father on the other, a coat hanger chiming discordantly between us, swinging on the just slammed frame.

Having retreated from a brutal assault to his senses – the sight of his sixteen-year-old daughter swaying in the dark like a depressed polar bear, her slack-jawed mastication of Hubba Bubba gum, the blue-cheese smell of her tennis-socked feet – his grim forebodings began.

I'd searched for him through my curtains only minutes earlier. He'd been sitting, as he always sat, at the wonky pale-blue table in the centre of the garden, on the grass he had just cut. He'd taken his shirt off to make the most of the day and he had his new swimming trunks on: navy, draw-stringed and unintentionally trendy – the word Nike embossed in large letters along the leg. They made me feel sorry for him; I didn't understand why. His index fingers beat away at the worn keys of his typewriter like neat mahogany hammers, ceasing only to retrieve a white handkerchief from his pocket to wipe sweat from his head, which was as shiny and bald as a burnt saucepan. Having established his whereabouts, I'd dive-bombed happily back to bed.

But my father moved efficiently with his swift, lean legs, and his soft-soled espadrilles made no sound on the stairs. If I hadn't been singing with such gusto, I might have heard the crack crack of his knees as he advanced.

'You silly goose!' may sound like a harmless enough sort of expression, even endearing when used with a certain intonation, but no three words could have struck more terror than these when they came from my father and were being used to describe me. 'I wouldn't mind if you were stupid!' he'd say to the door before counting the days until my Leaving Certificate exam as he padded back down the stairs and out to the garden again. Sixty-five, sixty-four, sixty-three, sixty-two. I listened to his voice fade and turned my music back up as it disappeared.

The dysfunctions of our family were heightened by living in semi-detachment from a beautifully functioning one. The Hamptons next door liked each other, they had hobbies, they liked the outdoors. Two boys and a girl, a Mum who loved Dad, all dark-haired, all the right weight. Nothing illegitimate, no runts of the litter, no stammerers, no cone heads, no bow legs, no lazy eyes, no harelips, no wing-nut ears. The hair on each head was naturally chestnut, skin on bones blemish free and softly honeyed.

While we were locked into the back yard, contained by our parents like prisoners of war, standing on each other's heads, flinging tap shoes at our brothers or pulling our knickers down to scare them so they'd stop giving us knuckle punches and Chinese burns, the Hamptons could be heard throwing a rugby ball to each other over the fence: 'Good shot, Conor!'

'Why, thank you, Sean!'

Back in our garden, the Frog, who'd been reading about Blondin the famous French tightrope walker, was frozen on the wall in Pie's ballet pumps, the washing-line pole for balance, and some leopard-skin underpants in the fashion of Charles Atlas. Sagging from a rusty hook beneath him over as far as the apple tree was some rope he'd salvaged from the garage.

The sun had gone and Pie and I had sausage-rolled ourselves up in picnic rugs to stay warm, squinting at clouds to see when it might reappear. A different sun shone over the Hamptons' house, a soft and perpetual one. They didn't need to look for it, it followed them as they laughed and ran, smoothing over their skin.

Aware that he now had our full attention, the Frog edged his right foot forward. As he lowered his left, the rope wavered dramatically, before rising up towards him. He sidled along another few inches, wobbled, slipped, scissor-legged, the rope catching him where it really hurt, swivelled one hundred and eighty degrees, and landed on his head with a nosebleed.

On a rare hot day, as I lay doused in vegetable fat and wrapped in tinfoil on the tarred roof of Saint Killian's school for boys, which was just behind our house and could be reached by traversing two broken-glass-topped walls and the chestnut tree where Ollie had his club house, Alison Hampton bounced around a tennis court. Pony-tailed, Vaseline-lipped, make-up free, her Lacoste skirt kicked up as she served to reveal just a peep of perfectly white knicker against warm brown skin; one side of pant caught in the cheeks of her bum as she bent over to pick up a ball, exposing its soft, cotton-wrapped cream.

I won tennis matches in my head, and practised my serve in the back garden in the dark. Once my toss was right I'd wallop balls as far as the shed, sending cooking apples flying from the old tree. Then I'd gather them up – using one of several neat little manoeuvres I'd mastered – transport them in a whiskey basket, take up position at the far end of the garden and start again. I didn't stop, even when a large flap of skin had come free

on the fleshy part of my palm and was purpling underneath. *Fame costs*, I reminded myself, *and right here's
where you're gonna start paying, in sweat.*

I lay supine on that roof while Alison collected her
trophy. You could have made a cardboard cut-out of my
body, my arms, legs, fingers and toes were stretched so
wide and taut for an evenly distributed suntan. Sitting
down for tea that night was agony, and that was before
a whack from Ollie on my fat, furnaced thigh.

I spied on the Hamptons through a small aperture in
the playroom window. I couldn't see them clearly with
my amblyopia so I assumed that they couldn't see me.
The window, which was smudged with finger-drawn
hearts and moons, opened just a couple of inches to
prevent any of us from jumping or being thrown out.
We'd squeezed a few of our cats through the gap over
time to test that theory about them landing on four feet.
I missed Sooty and Sweep.

When Mum tried to watch the main evening news she
unwittingly became a human shield. The Frog ducked as
Ollie threw an egg. It hit Mum and cracked and glooped
down the side of her face. While we were delivered
smacks on our backsides, fuelled with so much frustration that they lifted us right off our feet, Alison
Hampton was being hugged by her parents, homework
all ticked and done, before skipping off to the cinema
with her new boyfriend, Ben. 'Bye, Mum! Love you,
Dad!'

*

The subject options for our year had been German or Home Economics. I suggested to my father that in my future, quite possibly desperate, search for a husband, knowing how to make a shepherd's pie might just work in my favour. 'Ah my eye!' he said. Men would come and go but a foreign language would always stand by me.

My German teacher, Frau Fleischer, was motivated by her theory that, genetically speaking, I must possess talent for something, with my father being almost fluent at the language and my mother being good at lots of things. In the months leading up to my Leaving Certificate, she took to coming in to school at seven in the morning to work on my grammar and to extend my vocabulary beyond *Speckledy Deutsch* and *Heil Hitler*, smelling of sleep and breast milk.

I hated German; it sounded smelly. While Patsy and most of the rest of my class baked flapjacks and apple pies, I recited *fahren, fart, far, gefarhen*, und again! The only round peg in a roomful of squares.

With time running out before my exam and because I still could not grasp the future conditional, Frau Fleischer phoned my father to explain the gravity of the problem. Little did I know of the scheme that was being concocted as I rocked on spent springs above them singing 'Holiday'. Enter stage left, quick salute to my fans, several back flips, the crowd roars, a perfect split jump in the air.

My German exchange, Hubert, the only son of a friend of my father's, was summoned to Dublin. He had a toilet smell about him and a downy moustache rimmed with whiteheads. He was *ganz interesant* in rocks. Igneous, sedimentary, metamorphic, the lot. For the two weeks he spent in Ireland we journeyed around the country from one rock formation to another, over karst, by shingle, down terminal moraine.

My father was a cautious driver. We travelled haltingly and mostly on the hard shoulder when he was at the wheel, bicycles and pedestrians passing us by. Not wanting to waste time on these lengthy journeys, and because Hubert's English was near perfect, my father asked him if he would help to improve mine. He began by telling me to pronounce the word apple. 'Opple,' I'd say, despising them both. And Hubert, shooting my father a waxy little grin would say 'Nein, Bunty, eet's not "Opple" eet's "Epple".' Then my father would say 'Exactly, Hubert! Wunderbar!'

On one of these day trips, Hubert in the back, contentedly cataloguing his collection of rocks; me with my face turned away and jammed up against the door as far from him as was physically possible, I got the hiccups. They were triggered, I suspected, from an abrupt change to the lurching and limping progress our car had been making along the road – my father slamming his foot alternately on the accelerator and the brake as if total engine failure was imminent, making not just the car's occupants but anyone within a quarter-mile radius, nervous. Old ladies turned back at zebra crossings, children risked everything to retrieve a thrown ball. What had been up to that moment simply embarrassing and vomit inducing, was suddenly perilously dangerous;

at a busy junction where the traffic lights were out of order, rather than slowing down or stopping altogether, my father sped up and sailed through at considerable speed, without glancing in either direction, his gaze steadfast on the horizon.

The timing of my hiccups was unfortunate because we were in the middle of a 'silence competition' – a game my father had dreamt up to achieve a bit of peace when he had grown tired of our gabbling and so he could concentrate better on what he was doing. Whoever stayed silent the longest won fifty pence.

Convinced I was pretending, he ordered me to 'Stop that this minute!' When I didn't, because I couldn't, he leant back, eyes still fixed on the road, and took a few blind swipes at my knees. At first I giggled with frustration and with all the attention I was getting, but when I saw that vein on the side of his neck begin to throb, I tried in earnest to stop. I breathed in, in, in, in as deeply and as far as I could. Silence for a few moments, then a loud exhalation followed by what was, unmistakably, a hiccup and a rapid expulsion from my nose.

'If you do that once more, you can get out!' I held my breath again and tried to give myself a fright but neither worked. Our Fiat 131 came to a halt on the Stillorgan dual carriageway and I was ordered out and onto the pavement, a five-minute walk from home. As I hiccupped and wailed and the car inched away, I watched the back of Hubert sitting there, all upright, Birkenstocked and smug. I hated him. I hated them both.

I had no intention of spending another second with Hubert and refused to accompany him on a hike across the limestone region of the Burren. Ollie was dragged along in my place, livid and swearing revenge (I'd blackmailed him into going by threatening to tell Dad about the ear he'd just had pierced). I remained in Dublin, happily imagining wild gales and a certain German boy stretching over a precipitous cliff for a bit of rock he couldn't quite reach. Safe and cocksure on home ground, I hadn't considered the vulnerable position I was putting myself in by making an enemy of Hubert, in whose company I would have to spend a further two weeks, only this time I would be thousands of miles away, *auf Deutschland*, at the mercy of Hubert's whims.

I was so miserably homesick for the ten days I spent with Hubert's family in Munich that they didn't speak a word of proper German to me, with the bizarre consequence of my having to use my few words of German to communicate with the Hoffmanns, to which they would reply in English. In the evenings we ate dinner on the patio: Vater, Mutter, Hubert and me. I didn't recognize anything on the table. Hubert's mother pointed at each item with a brown, loose-skinned hand, further creased by a heavy gold watch. 'Heer ve habe black brot, gestrudellen, genoodlen, gedumplingen unt, how you say, wurst.' 'Tastes good, *ja*?' she'd ask after every mouthful, and while I privately negotiated a knobbly sausage or a bouncy bit of fish, Hubert's father would sneak up behind me and tie some trinket around my neck. Every morning at breakfast, I would find a purple or blue velvet pouch beside my place setting filled with gold bracelets and chocolate coins.

The kinder the Hoffmanns were to me, the more homesick and puzzled I became, until I accepted, with a degree of stoicism that both surprised and impressed me, that I must be dying. My parents had sent me to Germany for one final holiday to allow them to make the necessary funeral arrangements in peace. It was the only way to explain why everyone was paying me so much attention, why I was being bought presents for no good reason, why Hubert wasn't bullying me back after the way I had treated him in Dublin, why my father had seemed suspiciously sad when I was leaving. Not only was I going blind, I had a malignant inoperable tumour and wouldn't be around for much longer.

I was dying alone in a country where the chocolate was the wrong colour and the TVs had thirty channels but not one that I could understand, the toilet beside my bedroom wouldn't flush and when I got hungry I knew I couldn't help myself to some more Häagen-Dazs from the freezer.

My stomach was swollen with constipation: as she was showing me to my room Mrs Hoffman explained that as they were having some problems with plumbing, number ones were all right upstairs, but number *zwei*'s in the bathroom downstairs only, *bitte*. Mum's voice echoed and broke on my calls home from an open, air-conditioned hall. And when blood seeped, I knew it wasn't the end, but I didn't know the German for 'time of the month'.

Big Hitler hands shook mine, sandals with pulled-high socks walked through neighbourhoods that were *Sesame Street* clean, bicycles with baskets and bells pedalled by, all orderly, *alles klar?* All neat. *Die Menschen von* Munich queued with sensible satchels and rucksacks across cord-jacketed backs, for buses that arrived on time. Above them the cypress trees that cast shadows on cut grass seemed to know they were looking good. Little lederhosened boys swung from church bells at teatime. Even the vagrants in Munich waited for the green man to appear before wheeling their lives across the road.

At night I lay fading on one of those lovely square pillows on which you can fit not just your head but your shoulders and most of your back, tears sliding off my cheeks, thinking of all the things that I might have achieved (victory wave at Wimbledon, dueting with Billy Joel to the home crowd and, for my father, a master's degree in gravitational relativity) and how sad it was that no one could bring themselves to tell me that I was so gravely ill.

When Hubert's mother took me shopping and bought me a silver Sony Walkman, which was what I'd wanted more than anything in the world and had asked my Mum to buy me for two Christmases in a row, I thanked her before excusing myself and running to my bedroom. I stepped out onto the balcony and looked over the red roofs of Munich, as frail and brave as Beth in *Little Women*, my short life coming to a close. I could feel the fever coursing through my veins, the world closing in, the distance greater.

I was flown home to spend my remaining days with loved ones and to feed the cat one last time.

Small boys hung under the barriers at Dublin Airport to welcome home whomever, and a couple crumpled together in reunified joy. Beyond them, somewhat awkwardly, stood my parents. With bag and protruding pumpernickel, I trudged towards them. '*Guten Abend*, Bunty!' my father enthused. '*Wie geht's meine kleine?*' An expectant smile on his face froze as he awaited my reply *auf Deutsch*.

'Hi, Dad,' I mumbled, swiftly deflating his mood.

In these dying days, my parents seemed oddly composed; I thought it a little strange that neither of them attempted to carry my case. Slumped in the back seat of the car, I heard my mother mention that we needed to stop at the shops to buy some cat food. This normality felt deeply peculiar to me.

My demise went into remission. I recovered my strength over the following weeks and was deemed healthy enough to sit my Leaving Certificate.

Since there were just six months between us – an unfortunate accident of birth – Alison Hampton and I, though at different schools, sat our Leaving Certificate in the same year. My mother went to Mass every day during the two weeks of my exams. On her way back from church one morning, where she'd lit a candle and said several decades of the rosary for me, she bumped into Mrs Hampton. Ever positive about her gaggle of geese, Mum told her that I had been delighted with the French paper. It was true; I was delighted. I had read somewhere that you should trust the first feeling you have when you come out of an exam. It hadn't been a lengthy post-mortem, but my first feeling was that I had performed exceptionally.

Poor old Alison hadn't fared so well unfortunately, and had found the paper quite tricky, according to Mrs Hampton. She had been tired after all, what with her success at the Fitzwilliam Open the night before and having competed at the finals of the Leinster Schools Debating Society the day before that. She was really extremely worried about how the French exam had gone.

Alison came fourth in Ireland. I got an E.

For the Art practical exam I perfected my trademark clouds and sky – hoping they would be so exquisite that the examiner's mind would be temporarily transported from the everyday. Beside me, Patsy stifled laughter at my dreamy wash of blues and whites as she attended to her sculptural piece – a papier-mâché horse, who was having trouble standing upright he was so exceedingly well-endowed (there was chicken wire, newspaper and glue everywhere; it was destined to be hideous). At the table ahead of me, Joanna Blake was drawing her own shoe. Rosemary was collapsed over her desk, arm wrapped around her work as though we were all desperately trying to copy her. Sam Jennings, the best in the class, standing back from her desk, calmly, determinedly moved her hand across the canvas: sleeves rolled up, all the right materials, bangles jingling, smoker's breath.

I took a darker slant on my English essay. 'Killing

Time' was one of the prescribed titles and instead of the predictable old stuff about stamp collecting and going to the cinema with friends, I went for an original and literal interpretation of the words, writing five upbeat and practical pages about various ways of topping yourself – walking into the propellers of a moving plane, giving up eating, securing yourself to a rock at low tide, etc. I indicated where I had used a calculator during my Maths exam as requested (5 x 7 and 8 x 3) and pondered mathematical conundrums in my head such as whether a thingamajig should be measured in inches when it's flaccid or erect.

That autumn I was struck down by a more malignant and damning affliction than the one I had suffered in Germany: a place at a third-level institution beyond the Pale, described by my father as 'the worst university in Europe'. Here it was intended that I would further my study of the German language. *Naturlich*.

It may have been the worst in Europe, but it was the only university that would take me, and even then reluctantly – Arts and on the third count. I didn't want to go to university. My father had gone, and my brother and sister too. It wasn't up for discussion. I was going and that was the end of the matter.

Why couldn't he understand that I wanted to be something else: a tennis player, a famous musician, an artist, I wasn't exactly sure yet, I just needed to decide for myself. My mother, staying well out of it, suggested that if I could come up with a viable alternative it might make my argument stronger.

And yet I couldn't help privately fantasizing about the possibility of my life as an academic. A reversal of fortune and a scholarship to Oxford: there I would be, high up in an ivy-covered ancient stone building in autumn, above a neatly tended grass quad, head bowed at the window table of my simple corner room, engrossed in learning, hair tied back, soft but serious face. Glasses still, but only for reading. Striped scarf in college colours for the winter coming in, breath visible as I run across the quad on January mornings eager to get to my lectures on time, and later, earrings on and Vaseline applied and off to high-table tea, where I'd sit only too aware of the gaze of my English professor – a visiting lecturer from Harvard – who favoured olive-coloured corduroys and elbow-patched cardigans and had fallen hopelessly for me, reciting poetry as we punted down the banks of the Isis on Sundays.

The first person I encountered at the university's open day was a too enthusiastically jolly, born-again Christian who guided us around campus and grounds, striding ahead, flat-footed in sandals and socks, singing scouting songs. I saw her later poolside, voice echoing still, in a sleeveless fleece top and swimming togs; pubic hair like spider legs protruding around beef-red thighs.

Maynooth University was everything I hoped it wouldn't be: priests in belted slacks, single-bar heaters in common rooms with cottage-cheese ceilings, deep secrets and solitude, and mutterings of hangings in the graveyard. Students with cropped haircuts and black bicycles with baskets and black layers of second-hand clothes and black moods and curled, coffee-stained, stolen library books. Insomniac girls from Glasgow with digs above the mill, who hung huge knickers on clothes hangers and recited Nabokov's *Lolita* in their sleep.

I stubbornly refused to integrate myself into college life – as an ongoing protest against my father whose big idea it was in the first place and as a way of punishing myself for not having concentrated at school.

I dreaded walking into the packed canteen at lunch hour – the disorder and rowdiness, the tomato-soup heat. The pressure of having to order sandwiches from boards I couldn't read in the rush and steam of the kitchen, then having to find somewhere to sit amongst groups of students who all knew each other, sensing everyone's eyes on me, made me turn around and leave.

In spending so much of my time alone, I had unintentionally created that most elusive of qualities – an air of mystery. Patsy and I envied it in other girls. We talked too much and had opinions, ill-researched and knee-jerk, on almost everything, never allowing a thought to travel even once around our heads before it was out of our mouths and expressed. Mystery was a quality we would never possess. Yet at Maynooth I gave the impression of being a deep and silent individual with an obsessive interest in the notice board, always hurrying somewhere, forever searching for something I couldn't find.

I sometimes searched for the girl who had sat beside me at my first English lecture and had been normal and friendly. I hoped we could become friends and I kept a lookout for her for weeks after. Often I'd think I'd seen her – laughing in a group, rushing over the bridge to the library, but I wasn't confident enough of my sight to be certain, and was too shy and afraid to approach her and reintroduce myself.

On the second leg of my journey home in the evenings, as I waited to catch a bus on Nassau Street, I would peer over the wall into the hallowed grounds of Trinity College, lonely and full of envy. This was where I was meant to be, if only I'd had a mind like my father's. Gathered around the steps of the 'Pav', illuminated in the early evening sun, were slim young women with English-sounding surnames, shrieking, clinking bottles on freshly cut grass, their floppy-haired boyfriends in crew-neck sweaters beside them, with rooms on campus for parties and late night reading and affairs. Clear-headed, bright young things destined for happiness and success.

'How was your day, pet?' Mum would ask when I got home. I'd remind her of how much I hated that question, my voice weak and unsure from lack of practice, and close the door to my room.

I remember one lecture in my first year, something about a boy and a drum, where to my horror I was singled out – pen in mouth, clueless – by a booming, disembodied voice. Sitting second row from the back and with weakening eyes, my glasses were as good as useless: all I could make out was a vague shadowy figure moving about in the far distance. Assuming, being my father's daughter, that I would have some salient points to add to the topic being discussed, the voice addressed me. 'Are you with us today, Lucy?' it enquired, when I stuttered something inane, sending giggles rippling round the theatre hall. 'No? Girl beside her with her hand up.' This incident ruled out my attendance at subsequent German lectures and on week-days I generally stayed in bed. I would put my clothes on over my pyjamas and do a good impression of someone in a hurry until my father had left for work. Once I'd heard the front door shut, I would retreat upstairs, undress and jump back into bed. If Mum caught me I could easily convince her that a lecture had been cancelled or that I had a terribly sore throat. I chuckled to myself the first few times I succeeded in pulling this off, till my father came home from work early one day and the voice outside my door said the only person I was fooling was myself.

On a Monday morning, I took the 66 bus to my first-year German oral exam, tucked away downstairs at the warm part of the back. There was no weather to speak of that day, just uniform grey, like looking at the world through Tupperware. A man got on at Grattan Bridge. He was wearing a brown leather jacket that was gathered into pleats at the waist, and his hair, side-parted and slicked back, dripped generously over his head and ears, as if poured from a frying pan, except for a naked patch above his neck, on that bit where babies are bald.

There were many places he could have chosen to sit, places with space, windows to lean against, but he bypassed them all and squeezed in beside me, immediately too close, expelling old heat from his polyester trousers and dust particles from the seat. I tried to focus on my notes. It was useless. I pressed my head against the cold pane and stared out at the nothing strange.

I watched the city pass: blurred, broken-down buildings along the quays, houses half-demolished but not quite gone, others half-built but never finished off. The tall walls bordering the Phoenix Park, with its murders, men in bushes, afternoon tea at the zoo; the old orchard in Lucan where my father's father picked apples to sell; out beyond suburbia, past damp grey fields where crows hunched in empty trees.

Something brought me back. The rhythm of the bus had changed. Through the corner of my good eye I could see a square thing, a box of some sort, which the man beside me was holding on his knee. Below the box, a strange motion had begun – an agitation, vigorous, like the shaking of a ketchup bottle, a wet sound like smacking lips or moist fish. The seat shifted and came away from its back. I stopped eating my Dairy Milk; I was going to be sick. Sweat scent mixed with diesel heat and 'I love Bono' in the window dirt. The trapped reek of tan tights on red easy-wipe seats, earthy and salted like porridge wiped up in a used J-cloth.

The bus shuddered and started and stopped like a sick horse. I felt the push of his thigh as it spread against mine. Something like spilt Fanta was sticking to my shoe. Slowly, too scared to disturb, I turned back to the window. Outside was now a tunnelled laneway of pebbledash grey, dead flies on brown sills, chipped nursing-home pinks. By a breeze-blocked wall a tired woman in slippers manoeuvred her trolley around an upturned carton of milk.

The brakes sneezed as we slowed into Leixlip. A sudden sense of air around me signalled a space between us. As he got up from the seat to leave, he lurched forward with the spasmodic motion of the bus, then swung back at me like a drunk, steadying himself with a grab of my shoulder, using the hand that had been active beneath the box. The hot heavy weight of his damp flesh on mine made me want to smash the window beside me and run. Someone pressed a bell and the pressure was gone, but the fug stayed with me for the journey – around me, on me, inside.

7

Lovely eyes

I lay in the dark alcove under the stairs and tried to get clean. In an area of a house where you would ordinarily expect to find breeding mice, moth-eaten duffle coats, picnic baskets, mildewed swimming togs, burst footballs, warped tennis rackets, vacuum cleaners clogged with dust and hair, my father had lodged a bathtub. It had been installed, along with a toilet and washbasin, to facilitate his burgeoning family and was to be used exclusively by his children, which was just as well as only the very nimble and young could access it. It involved clambering in from the toilet seat over the adjacent bath taps, reversing, then carefully lowering yourself to lie beneath the roof, which sloped dramatically downwards and trembled when people climbed the stairs over you, scattering bits of paint and dead spiders into the bathwater below. Due to its limitations of space it could never be cleaned or serviced in any way. A makeshift curtain, fitted on a rail above the taps, had come free of some of its rings, and was further obscuring the light.

I closed my eyes and slid under. Cocooned in the grey tunnelling water, I was weightless, safe, warm. It had cooled to the perfect temperature. I wondered if those people – saints, sinners, infidels, plotters – who were boiled alive during the Spanish Inquisition enjoyed a few moments like that; a few moments when the water felt just right, balmy and pleasant, before it cooked them like meat.

I surfaced, and felt around the floor for the box of Clairol Nice 'n' Easy I'd bought in Arizona Brown. A simple one-step application, the packet said, with a new improved drip-free formula and a splash-safe plastic cape. I studied the boyish model on the carton: she was giggling about something while giving a slender-fingered flick to her cropped and gleaming hair, which was quite like a female version of Prince's – exactly the look I was going for, for the following evening's debs dance. 'Could you be the most beautiful girl in the world?' I sang to myself, applying the dye with gloved hands, ammonia singeing my scalp.

The water-wrinkled big toe of my left foot operated the hot tap – the bath water had become tepid and there was half an hour's development time to go – it spat out a few scalding spurts and then nothing. There must have been an airlock. I lowered myself back and kicked my legs about to keep warm.

Leftover tiles from the kitchen had been patchworked on the walls around me. In their marble I daydreamed, searched for faces in the patterns, the way you do with clouds. Sometimes I'd find a face like the devil watching me and once I'd seen him, it was impossible not to see him, there he was beside me – brows arched and furious

– there again over my head, Lucifer locking me from every angle with his horns. Was this a sign? Was God angry with me? I had done some immoral things recently, seen things I shouldn't have seen. Could I blame my fading sight for poor romantic decisions? I had given up wearing my glasses outside the house because my eyes were the one thing men seemed to like about me.

Sam had said they were a most unusual shade of slate grey just before he broke up with me, ending our three-week relationship. He'd said it wasn't going to work out because I wouldn't let him touch me upstairs and he was used to going all the way. Patsy, playing DJ, sat cross-legged on her bedroom floor sorting through albums for an appropriately gloomy song to play, her free hand pressed against her nose attempting to alter its shape. 'There's more fish in the sea,' she said as she put a record on the turntable, lowering the needle gingerly. But what did she know? She'd never been in love. She was still having crushes on female teachers and confessed to a dream she'd had of becoming stranded in a log cabin in Switzerland and being suckled by our monstrously bosomed Geography teacher – a perverted fantasy that would provide excellent fodder for future fights.

I rocked and sobbed to 'She's Out of My Life' while Patsy, relishing her role of comforter – how much less complicated it was to be a best friend when things weren't going according to plan – got out of bed each time the song ended and lifted the needle back to the start so I could sob through it all over again.

I swore I would never love again but that was before I met Frankie. I'd been at the triangle in Ranelagh squinting over the road at the window of Abrakebabra, when his bicycle collided with mine. I had been trying to establish whether Shane had started his evening shift; he'd been promoted to manager of the Ranelagh branch and I'd figured that if I couldn't have Sam, with a full year having passed since our break up, his twin brother would be the next best thing. I was also getting a little desperate – my debs dance was less than two weeks away and there was no Prince Charming in sight.

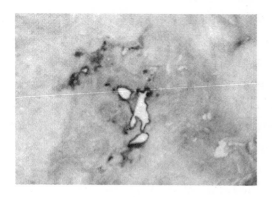

Once we'd untangled pedals from spokes, I asked the stranger whether he could see someone of Shane's description behind the counter. He said he couldn't be certain, but it looked like a woman at the till. And that's how it started; we got talking and he asked me to join him for a drink. I liked that he was from Nigeria and was far too old for me. He wanted to be a famous actor, just as I did at that moment. Both of us were waiting for our big break, but Frankie knew people in the business – with my beautiful eyes I'd be bound to get work, he told me, and promised to make some calls.

After several dates around the bars of Ranelagh he invited me back to his flat and was on top of me before the kettle had boiled. No, no, I wanted to keep my polo neck on. We weren't in the bed, but beside it, on the floor. I'd had too much to drink; now horizontal, I had the sensation of falling backwards into a vortex. He didn't undress, just pulled his trousers and underpants to his ankles as though he were on the toilet. There was none of that foreplay I'd seen on TV; he was straight in with a painful shove. I watched his face as he worked – he wasn't looking at me but beyond, with an expression of focused determination. He had the sort of nose you could see right up; black nostril hairs hardened with mucus. A globule of sweat quivered on the tip of his nose as he moaned. He wrestled out of his shirt – a waft of meat-smelling sweat and tiny spots like goose pimples across the chocolate skin of his shoulders – causing the droplet of sweat to fall onto my lip. So this is what it was, this was what sex felt like: the push and back movement of a lawnmower on grass.

I was moving backwards across the floor as he continued into me. The sober part of my head was saying I shouldn't be there, but his weight bearing down was too forceful to fight, as was the thought of the main thing: I had secured a boyfriend and partner for my debs. We would arrive together at the Burlington Hotel where everyone would eye me enviously with my exotic older man. I would be popular; people would be impressed. Everyone would remark on how I'd blossomed since leaving school, speculating about where I'd met Frankie, how we must have been studying at the same university.

I focused on the things I could see under the bed: a laundrette-sized box of Omo washing powder, the plastic rings from a six pack, a scrunched box of John Player Blue – which always made me think of the Stardust fire – a crust of toast on a plate. Finally the mowing stopped. He rolled off me and lay on his back, breathing hard, done.

Church bells rang as I made my way through Donnybrook the next morning – dazed with stale drink and lack of sleep, a packet of Tayto in my shaking hand to help the hangover – and climbed in the downstairs bathroom window and back into bed. With time to think, I got worried and guilty, the day-after-the-night-before blues: I shouldn't have done it. Could I be pregnant? Why hadn't he kissed me goodbye? Nothing had happened, that's what I'd tell Patsy. My face stung from abrasion, there was dirt under my fingernails, my new polo neck was stained and stank of cigarettes, the throbbing pulse at the base of my head wouldn't let me forget.

'Lucy! Frankie's on the phone!' Mum shouted from the bottom of the banisters, unaware that I was less than five yards away, in her telephone voice – commanding enough to travel three flights of stairs, yet sweetly affectionate, should the caller be listening.

There was still ten minutes' development time to go but I felt for the plug chain with my feet and yanked at it between my toes. As the water drained I stood up and leant over to the bathroom mirror to see how my hair was coming along, wobbled on my return and left a gloved imprint of my hand above the towel rail on the wall.

Frankie is on the phone. Could there have been five more perfect words? I clambered back out across the obstacle course of bad plumbing, cursing as I watched the bath water leave great dirty tidemarks in its wake, dye globules dripping down my back and onto the carpet below. I thundered into the kitchen, my still-attached cape blowing up and trailing brown along the walls, trying to compose my thoughts. I had waited a full seven days and six hours for this phone call – nagging Ollie to get off the line so Frankie could get through, finally phoning Patsy to analyse why he hadn't rung from every conceivable angle.

The telephone was the single most important object in my life. I was partly terrified of it – it made my stutter worse, made people confuse me with a boy, obstinately refused to ring when I prayed for it to – yet I was completely dependent on it. It was in the kitchen, family headquarters, so there was never any privacy. Our father would roar and tut from the kitchen table while we tried to make arrangements with friends, correcting our accents, our choice of words, the way we were standing, badgering us to hurry up because we were costing him a bloody fortune.

He loathed the invention and used it for two purposes only: emergencies and to tell his best friend jokes, his laughter so riotous it made us giggle along, though we wouldn't have a notion of what the joke had been about. Otherwise it was another source of ceaseless disruption – oddballs intent on making his life a misery. When it rang, even if he were standing right beside it, he would holler 'Telephone!' through the house, summoning one of us, usually my mother, who would come charging downstairs, wrapped in a towel, bath suds clinging to her red ankles. To my mother the telephone was a vital means of communication, conversations were to be enjoyed and shared. Her eyes latched onto whoever was in the kitchen with her whenever she was on it, so she could entertain us, and the person on the other end of the line, simultaneously. She was equally involved in our phone calls and always listened openly, often adding her tuppence worth.

Frankie told me he couldn't come – something about not having a dress suit to wear. It didn't register; the adrenalin was still flowing from the excitement of receiving a call from a boy. I was concentrating on choosing each word carefully. The attitude I was aiming for was one of cool indifference. 'Not to worry,' I said. 'No problem at all.'

I imagined myself into the painting of the storm, howling, inconsolable. My taffeta dress hung in readiness on my wardrobe door with the scarf Mum said would finish it off draped across its hanger in illustration. When Pie got home from her Liturgical Movement (she did them once a week, danced around an altar to hymns in a sheet) and saw the condition I was in, she phoned him back to say that God wouldn't forgive him for ruining such an important evening in my life. I struggled with my faith that night, though I didn't dare question it aloud, just in case He might be listening.

When Mum told my father of my misfortune the following morning he was already in poor form; she'd brought it up while he was writing her another ruddy housekeeping cheque. She always talked too much while she waited for cheques to be signed to distract him from what he was doing before he changed his mind. When it came to requests for money, the safest way to approach my father was to put it in writing – the way Ollie did when he needed new tennis shoes – a rational, well thought-out request expressed in his best joined writing. The direct approach was a brave but risky alternative.

With chequebook in hand he cursed at the prospect of the utter misery of the evening ahead, which he was now dreading all the more (it was traditional at our school that parents attend the dance and slip off at the end of the evening to give their daughters a few hours of freedom): show-band music, microphones squeaking with feedback, soapy mashed potatoes, the possibility of being dragged up to dance by Joanna Blake's mother as had happened at a recent wedding. She'd been on her way back from the loo and a little worse for wine when she pulled my father onto the floor to waltz, the back of her dress caught in her tights. There should be a word for this phenomenon, which I'd seen at least once before

– 'confabrication' perhaps?

And there would be his misfit of a daughter: home-dyed hair, feathered, fulsome and moussed into place; legs like a cowboy's coming out of a blue satin dress, blue to match her eyes, now tiny and raw from rubbing; and collecting, through piteous applause, a clay tile. Designed by her Religious Education teacher it would be inscribed with some profound motto such as: Live for today, learn from yesterday, dream of tomorrow.

But Paddy from the Liberties loved me, Paddy climbed drainpipes for me. My father stayed in his study or set off on a brisk five-mile walk to the yacht club whenever he called around. I loved that he was unemployed and had even less direction than me. I made him my social experiment. I encouraged him to get a job and to take up Italian. 'Italian my eye! How about someone who can speak English for crying out loud,' I heard my father say to Mum. And the more my father disapproved, the closer Paddy and I became.

When I wasn't let go to a fancy-dress party that Hallowe'en because I'd been caught borrowing some limited edition fifty pences from my father's coin collection, Paddy climbed the drainpipe two storeys to my room. I woke the following morning to find him at the foot of my bed and dressed as a leprechaun.

Mum came in all fresh and humming to wake me and found the two of us under the covers. I kept perfectly still, as though in deep sleep, Paddy beside me snoring, and followed her movements through my lashes, the way I used to when she pretended to be Father

Christmas, tip-toeing across the room and very, very gently placing a sock stuffed with chocolates and an orange on my bed.

She backed out and closed the door quietly, as I knew she would, avoiding anything awkward. As soon as I heard her footfall on the stairs, I kicked off the covers and ushered Paddy back out the window, lambasting him for giggling and petrified that my father might appear. I felt defensive on Mum's behalf, mortified that I had been caught in this situation. I wanted to explain to her that nothing had happened, that I hadn't invited him over, that he had arrived in the night and we had just fallen asleep together, all of which was true. We never spoke about it – neither of us could have sustained the mortification of a conversation about safe sex – but I knew Paddy's days were numbered.

I shouldn't have done it. I couldn't remember his second name but in that fuzzy, six-pint, end-of-night sight, Paddy's best friend Skello went from being small, ginger-haired and not my type at all, to really quite attractive from a certain angle. We stumbled back to his place and I fell into his bed; he curled up with his collie on the sofa playing hard to get.

That night I dreamt of a wall, a wall too big for me to climb, and on the other side, a porcelain toilet. I woke early with an aching head and a clammy sensation between my thighs. I felt the damp sheet. I turned the mattress over, panicking, stuffed the sheet in my rucksack and snuck out past the sleeping carrot top. I went back two days later to return the washed sheet. It was one thing being a seventeen-year-old bed-wetter but I didn't want him to take me for a thief. I told him I'd spilt some water on it. Like he believed me.

And then there was Valentine. No, after Skello there was that doorman from The Bailey, and then there was Valentine. Valentine Wentworth had just the nine fingers and was of no fixed abode. He spoke in a raspy whisper at the best of times but would become hazy-eyed and mute if you asked him about the missing digit. Not that anything happened between us. Nothing happened, we shared some curry fries that was all. He turned up at our front doorstep for weeks after and Mum took him for a tramp. She fed him breakfast and christened him Long Hair. A perfectly attractive trait in most people, but when she used those two words together they recalled oil-slicked licks dripping on mohair.

Troy had all his fingers intact but the most unbelievably smelly feet. The lead singer of Lost for Words, his hair hung like brackets around his face and there was little to say in between. Much of our brief relationship was spent tugging his cowboy boots off so he could steep his feet in the washing-up bowl from the sink. He'd sob uncontrollably whenever he heard 'Stairway to Heaven'. The other odd thing about him was that he ended all his sentences with the word 'but'. I liked this quirk, found it endearing, until I read in the papers that three children, semi-feral from having been locked in a basement by their deranged mother for eight years and deemed by psychologists severely damaged for life, all had this trait in common. They all ended their sentences with the word 'but'.

But Baba, a devotee of Krishna, had beautiful feet – he wore open-toed sandals year round – and strange white sumo wrestler-type underwear. Was it OK for a Catholic to be with a Krishna? I wondered what God would think. He was very clean, ran a bath each time he went to the toilet and used the dip under his rib cage for his soap. We spent hazy afternoons in the Iveagh Gardens making daisy chains when we weren't searching for magic mushrooms at the Hellfire Club, an ancient ruin on the lower slopes of the Dublin mountains that we visited on weekdays when I pretended to be at university. Heads in the sky we'd freewheel all the way home, me on the crossbar of his black bicycle in his ankle-length Afghan. He used to take me to a vegetarian restaurant; I called it the Golden Abattoir because it made him laugh. But his mantra became monotonous and he only liked me when I was happy, when there were positive vibes. I was too grumpy too often, he said. He didn't understand that that's the shape my face makes in repose.

Through Baba I met a toothless junkie – it was where he sourced his drugs. The trick of neon club light gave him a silvermint smile but when dawn broke there were gaps in his teeth and it was in those gaps that he stored his dope, concealed in cellophane. When I swallowed that five-spot he asked me to mind, a mini version of myself watched from the ceiling for three days. Everyone did. They all watched me on the 46A. As soon as I turned round they all turned away, pretending to be busy wiping steam from windows.

The night I met the Olympic canoeist I was in a foul mood. I'd mistaken two strangers outside Bewley's for Patsy and Rosemary; I'd waved at them and broken into a half-run before I realized it wasn't them. My hair wasn't right either. The man in Peter Marks had misunderstood me when I'd described what I wanted – a mohawk – and he'd given me a mullet instead. Patsy, Rosemary and I covered the radius of the city centre in search of the Nomads – a group of southside ne'er-do-wells with Dublin 4 addresses and jobs – Kehoe's, Grogan's, Hogan's, the Long Hall. My feet were bunched into my Doc Martens and pinching – they were the only pair left when I'd bought them and were two and a half sizes too small. As I walked I worried that my toes and feet might merge some day into two misshapen humps, like the ones those Chinese women have, but consoled myself that at least they were a sign of beauty somewhere. When we finally tracked them down in The Globe – all casual and fancy meeting you here – it was last orders at the bar.

The Olympic canoeist, a cousin of one of the Nomads, had a bed that had seen so much action it tilted sharply towards the floor. I had to hold myself in at night, sort of strap myself in with the sheets, feeling seasick. He rode on top of me six times a night, calculating how many calories he was burning as he worked, then up Leixlip river in his kayak at first light, all steroids and sweat, top-heavy arms chafing his chest as he went, two wiggly legs trying to hold him up downstairs.

Every day was an Olympic-sized challenge for him. Cut across him at the bar and he'd rise up with aggression like a bear, but in the company of women he fancied he was considerate and meek, like a 'new man', folding pieces of toilet roll into neat little squares before dabbing the end of his manhood.

Abandoned one morning, I balanced in the listing bed – hung-over, make-up smeared, smelling of sex – and felt around for the remote control. I dully flicked through the channels, nothing on: cartoons, Mass, football, Mass. The layout of the church looked familiar. I sat up, tickled when I recognized Alison Hampton and her family sitting in a tidy row and Father Perry preaching from the altar. The cameras panned to the next reader approaching the podium: a woman in a tweed suit and scarf making self-consciously slow progression. Shoulders back, chin slightly raised, she adjusted her microphone, and in an accent more Anglo-Saxon than ever, my mother began reading. I got up and ran myself a bath. What was I doing with my life?

And how long had I been seeing my boyfriend, Doctor Nugent asked from behind the curtain as I bent forward on the taut white sheet of the check-up bed. I'd gone to see him with the excuse of a verruca but actually to get the morning-after pill. He told me a girl of my age should regularly check her breasts. Is it serious, he wanted to know as he unhooked my bra. Lie down now, that's it, he said as his hands explored my chest then travelled south to open the top button of my jeans. His fingers pressed under my navel exploring some more, breath wheezing through his nose hair too near.

Who else was there? That guy with the full-sized tattoo of Neil Diamond on his arm, the one with the brown eyes I'd flirted with in Kehoe's, only discovering as we got up to leave, that he hadn't been sitting on a chair all evening, but was four foot five on his feet. Patsy's brother, Oscar's best friend who kissed me at that dance in Dingle, then sat me down next day and broke it off very gently because there was someone else he liked more. Patsy said she was pretty sure it was illegal in the first place, considering he had just turned fourteen.

8

Lovely girls

I'd had enough of Alison Hampton. Enough of her terrific exam results, enough of her marvellous tennis achievements, enough of how her long, slender neck brings 'Madonna dal Collo Lungo' to mind, enough of how I should keep my forehead still like Alison does when she speaks. The very sound of her name had begun to irritate my ears – A-li-son – so proper and pretty and sweet. Lovely girls like Alison are always bestowed with Christian names like Alison or Katie or Juliette.

I hated hearing her voice warbling over the garden wall when she came home from Oxford, where she was studying medicine, for Christmas and mid-term breaks. And yet when I heard it I couldn't resist taking up position by the window in the hall. Overlooking the side passageway of the Hamptons' house, it provided a perfect vantage point from which to spy, and, since Ollie had kicked a football through it, afforded views far superior to those from the playroom window, with distant and foggy squinting.

Ten years on and my father and Mr Hampton were

still on frosty terms because of that window. Having confiscated the football and come up with a suitable punishment for Ollie, my father had replaced the original stained glass with the cheaper alternative of plain glass. When Mr Hampton complained that having such a window overlooking the side of their house was an invasion of their privacy, father had snorted, assuring him that we had better things to be doing with our time than monitoring the comings and goings of the Hampton family. The Malones came over for dinner one evening shortly afterwards and peered immediately out the hall window when they were told about the scrap. At that very moment Mr Hampton happened to be passing below and, sensing he had an audience, his eyes were drawn instantly up.

The row of hastily planted Leylandiis made it a little more awkward but from a certain angle it was still possible to spy. I watched as Alison set off on a walk with her mother the last time she was home: arms linked, talking animatedly, oblivious of my lazy-eyed gaze. Mother and daughter always appeared locked in some form of embrace; they probably couldn't even watch TV without tickling each other's toes or making plaits of each other's hair. They were similarly tall and bore a strong resemblance to one another: Mrs Hampton had kept her figure neat through years of playing doubles down at the tennis club and she wore her chestnut hair in a manageable bob. They shared clothes and laughed about the same things with their big apple-advert teeth. When people commented that they looked like sisters, they'd giggle and say they were more like best friends.

Alison was dressed down in her casual gear. How I hated her elfin face in that Afghan-style hat, the way her pert breasts stood to attention under that cashmere sweater, the curve of her backside in those freshly creased jeans, that freckle-faced smile on her make-up-free skin.

On rainy Sundays Alison and her mother made pavlovas and flans and Alison's speciality, chocolate brownies, for coffee mornings, cake sales and for their next-door neighbours. Cooling racks of leftovers and new recipes were delivered to our door while the Hamptons, who never appeared to eat their own baking, sat back and watched us grow as the months passed.

Alison was the sort of person who could manage just two squares of chocolate at a time; the remainder she would store in the fridge for another day. I pictured the inside of the Hamptons' fridge. There would be no evidence of unhealthy relationships with food: no low-fat toffee yoghurts, no I can't believe it's not butter, no congealing bowls of Weight Watchers baked beans. It would reek instead of German sausages and expensive cheeses and jangle upon opening with the bottles of champagne chilling in anticipation of the next event to celebrate.

Mum said Alison was quite the cook as we swarmed around the kitchen table feasting on her brownies, Pie eating hers with a fork to appear less greedy, me with a mouth too full to reply, in my Peruvian-style hat which gave me the look, not of a lovely girl, but of someone on day release from a care facility.

Alison was up early each morning of her holidays to make the most of the day; college breaks were no excuse for sleeping in. When she wasn't baking or enjoying the fresh air or visiting garden centres with her mother, she was winning tennis tournaments or climbing mountains in Wicklow with Ben. Despite living in different countries they were still going strong; her first-ever relationship was serious and long-term.

It couldn't have been much later than nine in the morning when I heard the crunch of wheels on the gravel next door and hurried to my observation post: Ben was jumping from his Range Rover. He didn't do anything slowly. He travelled at a trot, the way small boys do, out of sheer enthusiasm for life, his tanned fists clenched above bulky thighs, his shoulders solid and round. Physically and psychologically he wasn't unlike Alison's brother, Conor. I mused over the possibility of inbreeding.

Before they set off for the hills Ben ran in to see Mr Hampton. He had something for him – what was in his hand? They got along famously, Ben and Alison's Dad. He insisted that Ben called him by his first name, Bruce. Alison had begun calling her father by his Christian name too – they were both adults now. She stretched to catch the car keys Ben threw as he went, revealing a shadow of space between the material of her jeans and the taut skin of her navel. No imprint of buttons, no strain, no folds of midriff on view.

I considered my own midriff in my Damart thermal pyjamas. They had been a disappointing purchase. I'd bought them in an attempt to appear virginal and wholesome, like the woman on the packet who wore hers with an oatmeal cardigan and slipper socks. Ollie said I didn't resemble a virgin as much as a bandaged survivor who had sustained 80 per cent burns in a fire.

I liked to fantasize about what went on behind the lemon-sherbet front door of the Hamptons' house, the dark underbelly of their existence. The secrets in the cellar, the bottles smashed in rage, the hair yanked from heads, the knives thrown, the incestuous relationships, the excrement smeared over walls.

Muffin getting stuck on the balcony outside Alison's bedroom provided the perfect opportunity to snoop. I was amazed that she had made it up there in the first place – a recent collision with a car had left her immobilized from the front paws back. I suggested a trip to the vet as we watched her drag her back legs and tail behind her through the garden gate. Mum said she was going away to make herself better, that's what cats do when they're sick. Translated what that meant was that under no circumstances was my father going to fork out for the vet's bill to have her put to sleep.

Mr Hampton answered the front door, eyeing me as he always did – quizzically – as if he knew he'd seen the face before but couldn't quite place it. He looked the same as ever in his canary-coloured golfing jumper, corduroy trousers and boating shoes. I followed him upstairs; he took each flight at a sprightly pace, his full head of Grecian 2000 bouncing about as he went.

The darkness and hush around the upstairs landing made me worry that someone was dead. In a whisper Mr Hampton explained that Alison's younger brother, Sean, was in bed with food poisoning. In the Hampton's house illness was taken seriously, not looked upon as an excuse to dodge work or school or as nothing that a good brisk walk in the open air wouldn't cure.

Alison was at choir practice – a talent I hadn't known about but that made perfect sense. Pie had a theory that you could tell what sort of singing voice someone has from his or her physical appearance. Being what my Granny used to describe as stout, I was an obvious alto. Alison with her equine features and slender figure would in all likelihood sing soprano.

Mr Hampton showed me to Alison's room but disappeared when he thought he'd heard poor old Sean call out from his sick bed. The window was already open: I climbed under it and onto the balcony and ferried my startled cat in. I surveyed Alison's room. The thick pile carpet was freshly hoovered; the floral eiderdown over her bed was tucked and pulled. On the shelves above were orderly rows of books, labelled photo albums, tennis trophies, framed photographs and newspaper cuttings of Alison receiving different prizes and awards.

Even the clock on the wall looked tidy, as if someone had moved the hands from twenty to seven to seven o'clock just to neaten them up.

I didn't have a free hand to explore, encumbered as I was with my paralysed, incontinent cat, but I imagined Alison's underwear drawer to be full of simple white Sloggies and pretty bras in pinks and chalky blues – no hipster shorts, no thongs, no turkey fillets, no Wonderbras. Alison didn't have a cleavage, nor did she pretend to.

The mirror behind her desk was peculiar. It was almost impossible to see yourself in it for all the super-imposed Post-it Notes and timetables of study and things to remember about medicine, tennis, debating, ambition and success. On her desk there was a hairbrush and some inexpensive moisturizer but no other suggestions of vanity.

Occasionally I would see Alison down at our local pub. With her Renault Clio parked round the corner, she was only ever staying for one. I pictured her straightening herself in the car before she came in: the hurried application of Vaseline to lips; hair tied back in a loose ponytail or perhaps in a pretty chignon; the spray of something citrus behind each earlobe; the quickest of glances in the overhead mirror. In seconds she could achieve what took focused hours of curling, highlighting, concealing, revealing, blushing, brushing, buffing, exfoliating, scrubbing, waxing, polishing and painting for me to create: the natural look.

Close up her face was the sort you would never grow

tired of looking at; it was fascinatingly perfect. Her chocolate eyes were wide-set and wet looking, her skin plump and blemish free, as though the only thing she had ingested in her life was filtered water. Her two top front teeth crossed each other slightly but this made her smile even more infuriatingly attractive.

If we found ourselves in the ladies at the same time or ordering drinks from the bar we would talk, or rather I would tell her all about my latest misadventure, sensing my make-up crack around my eyes and lips, and she would listen and laugh. Alison rarely talked about herself. 'Enough about me, how are *you* getting along?' she would always say. I was a bewildering and fascinating creature to her. She was still getting great mileage from the night she had to treat me in Casualty. She'd been doing her student placement at St Vincent's when I had been delivered in with a suspected dislocated shoulder.

I'd been at a cousin's wedding in high heels I was unaccustomed to. As soon as the music began after dinner – a Frank Sinatra tribute band – Mum was up. Mum loves to dance, abandoning herself girlishly with all the right moves. Shedding pounds as she twirls, it's her favourite way to keep fit. This was another thing I hadn't inherited – an ability to dance. I never knew where to look, what expression to wear, what to do with my arms. I had only agreed to partner Uncle Arthur because of my fondness for old men and because Mum said something about him having won some sort of award, something about St Vitus's dance.

We took to the floor for 'New York New York', Uncle Arthur opposite me, paunch over trousers, doing the white man's overbite with his rubbery old lips. He seemed a little unsteady on his feet, but I was shaky too. Under my dress I was wearing one of those second-skin things to hold everything in and my thighs chafed together uncomfortably as I moved. I tried to talk over the music as we gyrated – I sang along with the words for a bit and had a go at that pointing thing people do with their fingers, stabbing the air above.

It was when it was over, as I was making my way, swiftly, before the next tune began, back to my seat, that I snagged the top of my shoe on an electric cable I hadn't seen and fell forwards onto the dance floor in what felt like painfully slow slow-motion.

Mum was telling Alison and the elderly lady in the cubicle beside mine about the gorgeous shot silk dress the bride wore, when the radiographer returned with my X-ray results. They indicated that my shoulder was strained but not broken. What he was concerned about, however, were the shadows on my left breast.

Mum and Alison smiled at each other, in that way that people do when they don't know what to say. The doctor, expressionless, suggested it would be best to have another look. The wedding chatter ceased, people talked over me, about me, in terminology I didn't understand. I was asked some questions about my medical history, the woman in the adjacent bed sat forward, listening in. The curtain was drawn around me. Alison led my mother out, suggesting she get some tea.

Left alone, I lay my head back and rested it on the pillow, tucking my feet under the hospital sheets. I felt absolutely fine; what was being hinted at seemed absurd. I wanted to escape from the sickness around me, to be out in the open air. There was no one to talk to and too much time to think.

A nurse helped me into a wheelchair a few minutes later and took me back to radiology. Everything and everybody was quiet. The radiographer indicated to a screen in the corner of the room, requesting that I go behind it and remove everything from the waist up so that they could get 'a really good look at my chest'. I unhitched my bra, listening to my own breath. How strange that my brain and body were part of the same thing yet my body couldn't tell my brain what was happening. This thought was interrupted by a mini-clatter of coins.

The second X-ray confirmed that the shadows on my left breast were not malignant tumours, clotted arteries, kidney failure, ingrown toenails, AIDS, gout, hepatitis A, B or C, but two fifties and a twenty pence piece – the change I'd stored in my bra when I'd got up to dance with Uncle Art.

I was 'a ticket', Alison told Mum as we left, 'an absolute hoot'.

I stood at the hall window the last time Alison was home, longing to see the world through her eyes: to have Alison's focus, to have a life that was going according to plan. I wanted to view life as she did: clean-edged and straightforward and defined. I wished my eyes were strong and working. Lovely girls like Alison Hampton don't wear glasses. Lovely girls like Alison Hampton see clearly.

9

One small step

Too distracted by advance homesickness to make rational decisions, I upturned each drawer from the chest in my room, making four separate clothes hills on the bed. I felt this malaise in the days before I had to go anywhere, a sour sensation in my stomach, a superstition of freak accidents and crashing planes; a fear that I would never return. I had talked of nothing else as I planned and anticipated this trip, longing for the weeks to pass when the day of departure was safely far in the distance, but now that it was inevitable, all I felt was an overwhelming sense of wanting to remain at home.

Left alone for half an hour that morning, I toured the bedrooms, quickly gathering the items on my list. For weeks I'd been deliberating about what I was going to borrow/steal: Ollie's beads, Pie's cross and chain, Dad's razors, vests and socks. I'd done a recce to see how much sterling there was in Frog's English money box (he had separate ones for dollars, pounds and lire), but it had been in vain; he made me a present of all the sterling he'd saved.

The dramatic shift in my family's attitude towards me was making leaving harder. Ollie, who had recently developed an interest in cooking, baked a cake on my final evening at home, the words *Bon Voyage!* inscribed across the top in wobbly icing. Mum returned from every visit to the shops with some travelling aid for me: a German-style money belt, four hundred Bewley's tea bags, an itsy bitsy reading light to encourage study, a packet of tissues – which she deemed an essential item for any trip – and, from my father, a suitcase on wheels.

As I rooted through the drawers of his writing desk looking for good things to take, amazed to find both this and the door to his study unlocked (a sign that he was becoming befuddled or had a misplaced trust in us?), the smell of its interior – old papers, damp wood, mixed with that scent of home – brought on another wave of melancholy. It was this unidentifiable odour of familiar things that made me wet the bed with homesickness as a child whenever I stayed overnight at a friend's. A phone call would be made to my mother, and I would be collected, instantly soothed by the scent of home she carried with her as she drove through the night in her slippers and dressing-gown.

My plump fingers and chewed nails smudging the face of a magnifying glass – protected by a velvety pouch, elderly and perfectly cared for – made it feel like an act of contempt. And perhaps that's what it was; I took it on impulse, with no idea of how or when I would use it. We'd had a few nasty run-ins over the previous months, my father and I, about not studying for my first-year exams, the Arizona Brown hair dye that had left its indelible mark on the bath under the stairs, the bottle of gin I'd consumed and cunningly replaced with tap water, my cavorting around with unsuitable, unstable men.

I finished packing, swapping my koala bear for a box of peroxide hair dye (I wasn't happy with the nickname the Nomads had given me – the Beetle – so I was going to experiment with blonde), my black and red-striped mohair sweater, my combat trousers and Doc boots, and a copy of my favourite song, 'Fairytale of New York'. I squeezed my koala back in, and zipped up the case. Filled with a fresh sense of excitement – my exams were over, I had a money belt full of notes, I was free for the summer – I tossed my bag down the stairs. Having exhausted all local and national possibilities, Patsy and I were setting off for London in search of freedom and future husbands.

The advert in *Loot* sought 'a dynamic, extrovert individual for West End company'. I circled it and charged down to the pay phone in the hall, taking the stairs two at a time. This sounded like a different and exciting way to make money. It suggested the possibility of some extra work in a movie perhaps, a fledgling's first opening.

Unless my boss, Mr Daisy Fried Chicken, physically deposited me onto main thoroughfares, which I travelled through at such breakneck speed – side-stepping the throng, ducking in doorways – that you might well have missed me, I stuck to side streets and alleyways between trading hours. 'Why Pay More?' it said on the ankle-length yellow and red sandwich board I donned, furtive and scowling, bottom lip pouting like a Mursi tribeswoman's.

We shared a one-bed flat in Nevern Place, Earls Court; Patsy and I and two Australian girls, two pillows, one sheet and a swarm of resilient cock-roaches who scuttled around saucepans in the kitchen sink and ascended our cleavages at night. When the time for talking had passed, we slept, we dreamt, of money, sex and men, till someone put Soul II Soul on and we did it all again: faces on, first cigarettes of the day stubbed out in last night's beer cans, deodorant-streaked smiley face T-shirts and silver-sequined hot pants and miniskirts donned, lipstick blotted on letters from home. Then downstairs past the sticky-floored communal toilet, its stagnant bowl water giving off a richly sweet stench, and up to Kensington Market we'd head, counting our tips and tugging our skirts to shield the spits from Muslim men on doorsteps of their whitewashed Edwardian houses chopped up into a dozen flats. Sometimes we'd pop into Pizza Hut on the way to see if they had any vacancies. If not, some garlic bread Supreme.

Jobs went and went that summer. Rain stopped play at Wimbledon, drenching abandoned mattresses on Earls Court roofs, sludging grey bitty rivers round huddles of butts, pit-pitting endlessly on blown Sainsbury's bags and sullying all those things that strangers leave behind: a set of wooden coat hangers, a face-down TV, sheets stuffed in a laundry sack, a naked Barbie – eyes round and wide, blonde hair knotted and muddy, like a victim of crime.

I could hear the smile on Mum's face when she phoned to give me my exam results: that nervous smile she uses when she has bad news to impart. Despite my attempt to turn the traumatic event on the bus to my advantage – I'd tried to explain what had occurred to the examiner, who insisted I did so *auf Deutsch*, which was a little tricky as the only sentences I'd prepared were *Ich spiele gern tennis* and *Wieviel kostet der Spiegel?* – I got a lousy 38 per cent.

As Mum tried to look on the sunny side, my father, in the background, issued last warnings and threats. Too furious to speak to me directly, he wrote letters throughout that summer that read like back-to-front ransom notes, insisting that I come home at once and get down to studying and that he would cover the airfare. In failing first year at university, I had done what he had considered almost impossible to do and this was my very last chance.

In an exam hall the colour of homemade orange ice-cream, I sat my repeat exams. The ghostly religious statues watching me from their high plinths in dimly lit corners, the pacing invigilator in sandals and socks, the freckled neck of the frantically scribbling redhead in front of me, all seemed to be saying, Too little too late. The few people I had got to know at Maynooth were passing exams and moving on without me, making my isolation even more complete.

With my exams failed I returned to London at the end of that summer having come to a mutual decision with the head of the German department that a gap year might be the most sensible way to proceed. My father hadn't ventured from his study since he'd seen my results and while I'd wallowed in all the lie-ins and deep baths that this cold-war tranquillity brought, I found it a little disconcerting. He had closed his study door very gently after our last fight. I was scared that he had given up on me; that I'd finally worn him out.

In the time it was taking me to complete first year, Patsy had graduated with a diploma in Public Relations. This felt like betrayal to me – I thought it was agreed that neither of us were bothered about studying or passing exams. She came back to London with me all the same, while she explored her career options.

Mum coerced my father into letting us stay temporarily at the cottage in Hampstead. He used the cottage as an office when he was in London, occasionally renting it out to visiting academics. He had been worryingly easy to persuade, telling Mum he'd washed his hands of me, that he was sick to his back teeth. Closing his study door behind him and with Mum clearing up out of earshot in the kitchen, he added that I'd put ten years on his life.

Patsy and I strode through the crisp leaves along Hampstead High Street. Up through the winding steps, steep and lamplit, along narrow rows of Regency houses, ochre-roofed and higgledy-piggledy set, some tall, some stout, like the sort of picture you'd find on an old-fashioned gingerbread tin. Past the smudged study lights of professional families, books piled high beyond velvet-cushioned window seats, cooks bent crooked in basement kitchens, cleaning lettuces in Belfast sinks. By an ivy-covered old man's pub with wobble-legged tables and men-only snugs, behind an austere Protestant church with locked doors, to a small terrace of whitewashed cottages, with shoe-scrapers and lanterns and porch covers, the last of which was my father's.

Following his initial seeming indifference to our staying there, my father had written and posted, in the scrawl of clear panic, some things for us to remember. Among the ten pages of instructions detailing where we might be most likely to bump our heads and how we should go about polishing the wooden table in the kitchen, was an underlined warning concerning the window shutters in the bedroom I would be staying in: *Note that fastening and unfastening the shutter catches entails leaning out of the windows. This may be hazardous for a short person.* He included a list of places of historical interest around the Hampstead area that we might like to visit – Keats house, Kenwood House, Karl Marx's tomb at Highgate Cemetery. We visited Keats Tavern on several occasions; the cemetery could wait.

Whispers of possible promotion to second-floor housekeeper indicated that my career in the hotel and catering industry was on the up. In the two weeks that Patsy and I had worked as chambermaids at the Royal Westminster in Victoria we had learnt some valuable tricks of the trade. To create the impression of a carpet having been hoovered, run a foot against the grain. Provided there are no obvious stains, sheets in a honeymoon suite can be smoothed over and de-creased, confetti kicked under the bed or flushed down the loo. Any money or chocolate in the vicinity of the bed, in fact anywhere at all in the room, you could safely assume was left there for you.

What no one had yet realized was that we were lousy chambermaids. While our largely Afro-Caribbean workmates set off for home having cleaned ten departures in an afternoon – remaking beds and turning mattresses over with one hand, or so it seemed – we would still be shoving our trolleys along corridors well into the evening, exhausted and complaining. If we found ourselves on the same floor near the end of our shift we'd lock a room from the inside, kick off our shoes and relax. If we happened to bump into each other earlier in the day when we still had some energy, we'd try on guests' clothes, jewellery, perfumes, parade before the mirror in their high heels and the hotel's bathrobes, and jump on unmade beds to the music on Capital Radio. We were going to be so much more than chambermaids – we had no intention of taking it seriously.

A bomb scare at the Royal Westminster sparked rumours of fresh IRA threats. A friend of Ollie's, a free-lance journalist, phoned to ask me about how it felt to be Irish in London at the time. No one said anything, I told him, but I tried to stress my 'h's when I needed more soap for room thirty-three. When a Tube stopped mid-tunnel and the lights flashed off, panic replaced impatience. Coming from the same country as Bono and Bob Geldof was no longer something to boast about, and no matter how many times I scrubbed them there was dirt under my fingernails.

When, inevitably, I was fired from the Royal Westminster, for refusing to pick pubic hairs from a guest's bath, this journalist took on a paternal role and took me out for a drink to help me consider my options. He had a friend, he said, at a travel guide publishers, Roads Less Travelled, who was about to start work on a new edition of their guide to Germany. With my knowledge of the German language, perhaps they could find a role for me. He said he would give them a call.

Excited at the prospect of working for Roads Less Travelled, I searched my father's bookcase for something I could study on German grammar that night. Along the top shelf was a miscellaneous collection left by tenants over the years: a baby name book, a pamphlet from the British Social Hygiene Council entitled *What Parents should tell their Children*, and a copy of J.D. Salinger's *The Catcher in the Rye*. I pulled this down, thinking of John Lennon and the inspiration it had been for the man who had murdered him, and became immediately absorbed. As I turned the page to chapter three, an envelope fell to the floor. It was in my father's careful handwriting and was addressed to a Mrs Marjorie Bastonme, my grandmother's married name. From the deep fold and yellowed sheets of the letter inside, it was clear that it had been wedged between the pages of this book for some time.

Each page of the letter had been numbered in roman numerals, and a wide space had been left at the sides for margins. It was unmistakably my father's writing, but it looked bolder and larger and was without the quiver it had recently developed. The letter began with him talking about how he was getting along at university in Mannheim – I knew that he had won a scholarship to study German there when he was still very young. He asked about how everyone was doing at home and admitted that he was feeling a little homesick.

At the start of the next paragraph was the point of his letter – a proposal. What he was proposing was to take a sabbatical from university, suggesting that he return to Dublin, perhaps live at home initially but with the intention of finding a job to pay his board and keep, and in a passionate plea to his mother, he begged to be let focus on his poetry.

I moved to the window and held the letter up against it. Wiping my glasses on my jumper, I tried to decipher the words that had smudged and faded in the folds. Heart thumping, I read on, hoping I wouldn't hear the sound of Patsy's boots on the stairs. This was an intrusion; a private letter from my father to his mother, it was like reading his diary in the dark.

Always self-effacing, he explained that he had written a few poems. They weren't bad, in fact some of them, he thought, were rather good and had been published in a university periodical, but the important point was that he had taken so much pleasure in composing them he wanted to devote a little more time to the discipline. Depending on how that went, perhaps he would take a longer break from university. He knew poetry wasn't something he could make a career of but – the letter finished mid-sentence. It had a stamp on it but had never been posted.

My father writing poetry was incongruous – I chuckled at the thought of it as I read through the letter again. I knew almost nothing about him; he didn't talk about the past, the way most parents do to bore their children. This letter was the most I had ever seen of him.

Did my lack of direction remind him of his own unfulfilled dreams? Did he resent my rebelliousness as something he didn't have the bravery to pursue? How afraid must he have been of his mother and unsure of himself to have not sent the letter?

I had a sudden longing to talk to him. Hearing his voice in the letter made me miss him. I had learnt more about him in those few pages than I had learnt in nineteen years of being his daughter but there were still so many questions. For the first time in my life I felt curious about him.

I put the letter back in its envelope and the book back where I found it on the shelf. This was something I should never have seen and I knew I couldn't mention it to anyone.

My mother told us we would have to leave Hampstead after two months of living there, because a Polish academic was on his way. I deliberated about whether to take the letter; deciding against it, I hid it in another book on the shelf and took *The Catcher in the Rye* with me. We went back down the hill. Down, down, down to a basement bed-sit in Gospel Oak, where we sat comparing navels and lives in a room with no view, a black and white portable TV, balanced on top of a washing machine and operated by pliers, and missing a sitting-room door.

It was in this scene of relative adversity, as I worked on my Roads Less Travelled application, that I grew to know the man who lived upstairs intimately: the full flow of his morning wee, his after-sex snore, his preference for

Countdown over *Coronation Street*. His favourite pizza was GoodFellas, on Saturdays he read *The Guardian*, and though I never met him, I glimpsed his purple duvet as it dangled from his bedroom window to air.

Patsy helped to dress up my dubious credentials, seeing how she could benefit vicariously. If I had a job at Roads Less Travelled, imagine the sort of edgy, creative men she might meet simply by knowing me. We had begun our hunt for husbands proactively; we'd even considered taking up rowing to this end, but the six o'clock start on Saturday mornings ruled it out, as did training in a dark indoor tank for four months of the year, and even then we would be in all-girl teams. Lately Patsy had taken to her knees at the liberal Catholic church down the road to pray to what our school head-mistress used to describe as God of the Gaps – the sort of God you only prayed to when you had a huge favour to ask.

After three weeks of preparation I presented myself for interview, a saleswoman with an empty suitcase.

10

Elysian fields

I opened my NiceDay spiral notebook and placed alongside it a felt-tipped pen in aquamarine, selected from a vivid array fanned on my desk like a peacock's plumage. The adjustment of my swivel chair caused the tower of Post-it notes I'd constructed to collapse. I re-sorted them into small, regular and large separate blocks, and assembled around me a box of bulldog clips, a NiceDay rubber, a hole punch, an officious-looking stamp thing, and five freshly sharpened pencils.

I was the only one in, all organized and early on my first day. I took a quick squint up my nose with my new pocket mirror – all clear – and applied a little more strawberry lipgloss. Beside my diary I put a tub of vanilla-scented hand cream (an excellent aphrodisiac, according to *Marie Claire*) and my lucky elephant key ring, well aware that its silver contrasted perfectly with the duck egg blue of my diary, particularly when set against my multivitamin drink that tasted like gripe water but came in a lovely chrome colour.

I shook my snow globe and watched sparkles of glitter whirl around my late cat Muffin's nose as I deliberated about where it should go. On the other side was a smiling close-up of me, flash-orange eyes but sufficiently distorted to make them appear more or less matching. With some double-sided sticky tape I affixed it to the top of my computer. Catching my reflection in its screen, I re-emphasized my side parting. I'd modified it from that morning's version which was a little too far to the right – Patsy said it made her think of that Conservative MP who sucked toes.

I hadn't quite figured out how to switch my computer on, having never used an Apple Mac before – a detail I didn't think worth mentioning at my interview, assuming it couldn't be all that different from a PC. In my in-tray was a file with 'Germany' typed across its spine; underneath, in bold lettering was written 'Roads Less Travelled Editorial Assistant, Lucy Bastonme'. The sight of these words was suddenly terrifying.

My grasp of the German language was tenuous enough but it positively shone when compared to my grasp of geography. I attributed this largely to the Geography teacher I'd had at school. Having read in dull monotone a passage about glaciers, for example, she would select someone in the class to re-read it from the start – invariably someone uncomfortable with reading aloud: a dyslexic, a chronic stutterer or me. Once they had blundered their way through the passage, the entire class would be instructed to read the same piece aloud but this time underlining as we went (the swots used rulers and pencils, the rest of us marked our texts freehand with whatever was about), resulting at the end of the year in an entirely underlined geography book and not a word of it committed to memory.

I ran through what I could remember: left hand is one with watch on. Sun rises in the east – think of yeast. It is the east and Juliet is the sun. North all depends on where you're standing.

The sitting position I'd adopted was a complicated one: left foot wedged under backside, right leg free and dangling, chest forward, elbows on desk, a face of centred focus propped on hands in between. I hoped to portray a combination of job commitment and avidity, hawk-eyed attention to detail, and a certain confident yet at-home casualness to my colleagues.

My new *Betty Blue*-style striped jumper smelt suspiciously of Patsy: Sure-smothered Saturday-night sweat. It was both too tight, creating a false but pleasing impression of ample-chestedness, and too short for me, ending just before my Gap low-rise jeans. Viewed from where I was sitting it wasn't a great look – midriff folded hamburger-like and hanging – but with breath held and upright I thought the effect was quite sexy.

A cramp was developing in my trapped left foot, but staff members had begun to arrive so I kept it where it was. Thumping up the stairs and through the swing doors they came with the cool morning air in flowerpot hats, ripped jeans, rucksacks, walkmans, suntans and sat-on-jacket smells.

I smiled broadly in their general direction – I couldn't make out their faces, but glasses were out of the question on my very first day and with this much potential.

It wasn't quite nine o'clock and I'd already gleaned two new facts. The one thing you should never do with the laces of runners is tie them. Whether you stuck them inside or cut them off altogether called for further research. The correct way to carry a rucksack was simpler – straps should be secured around one shoulder as opposed to the two-shoulder style I'd been sporting, there shouldn't be an orang-utan or octopus dangling from its zip, it should be not too full, not too empty, and should come in a muted shade of khaki, preferably, or a dull pigeon grey.

The fan on my desk was flirting with my hair, the stark sun making me sleepy. I drifted off and out the window into a soft-focus Covent Garden morning. On the pavement outside the Italian cafe an upended bucket of water diluted the weekend's excesses, causing a pigeon to flutter and land at the feet of a face hidden in the salmon-coloured pages of the *Financial Times*. With a clatter the shutters came up at Gap, exposing three naked mannequins and a window dresser's bent back-side. Awnings rolled down, wet pints of fresh milk were delivered, there was the listless tick of a waiting black cab. A toddler ran, fell, paused, cried. Out through the slamming barriers of the underground spewed shoppers, workers and shoplifters along with the stale Tube air. Through the lens of his new camcorder, a German tourist was catching it all.

When Roads Less Travelled's Managing Director Chris Somers interviewed me for the job – runners perched intimately on the edge of my chair, head at a tilt and resting on a sinewy fist – the expression he wore was one of being tickled, won over. Even as I hoodwinked him into hiring me, I'd visualized some future date when he would be sitting as he was that day, his head at the same tilt, but with an expression of weary exasperation washing over his face, if he could summon up an expression at all.

I told myself to concentrate as he explained what the position entailed. As assistant to Senior Editor Jack DeSouza, I would be expected to proofread travel writers' research, using my knowledge of German to double-check the use of colloquial phrases and words. I would liaise daily with writers, cartographers – whatever they were – printers and the production department.

Perhaps I should have told him at that moment that he was making a grave mistake. Perhaps that's what I would have done if it hadn't been the job I'd always wanted. Some people pack peas under hairnets in Hackney Downs, whereas I had secured a job at a travel-guide publishers in London's West End. Henna-haired girls with exotic upbringings and pierced belly buttons would befriend me. We'd link arms and kiss – not like lezzers, but because we were alternative and together – and sit cross-legged in damp corners of basement pubs and indie clubs, fingering roll-ups and spliffs with chewed nails. On winter afternoons you'd find us bitten-lipped and moody behind the steamed windows of the Dandelion Cafe, confiding in each other our painful break-ups, bulimic episodes and bumpy pasts, hands hugging coffee mugs beneath stretched cardigan sleeves. In the office I'd carve up the world and toss theories and basketballs about with shaven-headed and dreadlocked guys with cute nicknames and Calvin Kleins taut over delicious treasure trails revealed in mid-meeting stretches and yawns.

I phoned Mum to tell her my news. She was thrilled, she said, over the moon. Before hanging up she told me she was popping round to the Hamptons' to borrow their garden table – good news always infused her with energy – and I knew she would take the opportunity to tell Mrs Hampton all about my wonderful new job. Though the garden table in question resided in the Hamptons' back-yard, it belonged to us. Mum had bought it knowing that my father would have thought it an unnecessary extrava-gance, particularly when we had the perfectly good wonky pale blue one. She had come to an arrangement with Mrs Hampton that she would keep it in her garden, pretending it was their table, which my mother would occasionally borrow.

My father sent me a 1900 copy of *Baedeker's Handbook for Travellers on the Rhine*, tied tight with twine and wrapped in endless brown paper like a pass-the-parcel package. Along the margins he had written notes in pencil and had underlined places he had visited as a young man and some tips for English speakers when cycling in Germany:

Cycling is very prevalent in the Rhenish districts. A strong brake on the front wheel and a good lamp for night riding are indispensable. Some of the narrower streets may be closed to cyclists and restrictions are often made on the use of the wheel in public parks. In most cases a number plate has to be attached to the bicycle and the police have the right to demand the exhibition of the cyclist's club ticket or passport.

I would make my father proud of me. I was determined. I would work hard and truly concentrate. Maybe I had a keen eye for proofreading without being aware of it. Maybe I'd finally found my forte. My attitude towards him had changed in the days since I'd read his letter and I resolved to make an effort, when I was next home, not to do anything to upset him and maybe to spend a little time with him. It would be easier now that I was working for Roads Less Travelled; he was clearly surprised and pleased for me. The title Editorial Assistant, even though there were a dozen of us, sounded impressive.

My new career got off to an inauspicious start. To mark my arrival some senior members of staff invited me out for dinner on the Friday of my first week. The four days in between had gone swimmingly; I'd drawn up a carefully ruled and colour-keyed timetable of all the different regional accounts of Germany I was going to be proofreading, and had attended a meeting in the 'boardroom' (a wittily installed stationary caravan) where, being the new girl, I didn't have to worry about contributing. My phone had rung only twice, once when the guys in production asked me to join them for lunch, once when Carrie, the lanky-limbed and mellow Australian receptionist, called to say my First Direct credit card had been delivered by courier and could I pop up to sign for it at my convenience. I basked in the novelty of being considered bright. When I spoke my colleagues listened with gravity at the possible import of my opinions, instead of gazing off into the middle distance or worrying things from between their teeth.

I was more than a little nervous about the dinner at Khan's Balti House in Bayswater. I prayed that the table talk would stick to things I could comment on. I'd prepared several interesting facts about sequoia trees and three-toed chameleons, which I practised to myself and would bring up when the moment was right. But there was only so much I could contribute to a debate about the pros and cons of Thatcher's Britain, or anything whatsoever to do with geographical phenomena.

In the bustle and clatter of Khan's we sorted ourselves around a table. Jack sat down beside me, in a crisp Armani shirt, coiffed hair, high-waisted, centrally creased jeans and a soapy-armpit smell, reversing his Comme des Garcons jacket on the back of his chair so that anyone who happened to be passing might notice where it was from. Chris was directly opposite me, his smile defining his craggy, lived-in face. The top two buttons of his shirt were open to expose some gay-looking beads on a Brillo-pad of chest hair, which sounds a bit tacky but that night was the most exciting thing. Amongst all of those edgy, spread-legged, sun-baked, travelled men, I was even finding myself sexy in a warm flowing way that I couldn't fully understand.

But I wasn't happy about being the centre of attention; there were too many things that could go wrong. I was still too vain to wear my glasses and restaurants are hazardous places for the visually challenged. I was also a little uncomfortable about Julia Thistlewaite being on the other side of me. Julia had earned the title of safest pair of hands in Editorial, all the more impressive considering she had only one eye. She'd been opening a bottle of champagne at her twenty-first birthday party when the cork shot out and into her right eye, blinding it permanently. There was still a cornea of sorts there, but it was useless and dead, and cloudy like a cow's.

We small-talked as I dished chutney on my poppadoms but our conversation was awkward, halting. When Julia spoke I made myself stare straight ahead, to avoid the temptation of examining her dead eye. And all my sentences were suddenly starting with 'I've got my eye on ...' and 'Did you see ...' When I couldn't think of anything else to say I contemplated my aloo gobi, nodding, smiling or shaking my head with feigned exasperation at the conversations going on around me. I chewed each mouthful of food laboriously before swallowing in that polite way you do when you're not at home. When my napkin slid off my lap, I bent to retrieve it from where it had fallen at the side of my chair and felt the delicious heat of Jack's thigh against mine.

Still on shaky ground conversationally – the topic had shifted to a patent that had just been given for a genetically engineered mouse, a Mighty Mouse, to be used for cancer research – I sieved through my head in search of anything vaguely relevant to add and recalled a perfect fact that also concerned man's control of nature. I cleared my throat and took a few gulps of beer.

'Did you know that an extra second was added to time this year to make up for the fact that the earth is gradually slowing down?'

No one said anything. I straightened my napkin, cheeks burning. Then without looking up from his plate, Jack asked, 'Oh really, so how does that work?' I hadn't prepared for any sort of come back, the fact alone was intended to kick-start a conversation which I, having made my contribution, could stay comfortably out of. I said it was something I'd read but would need to go back to double-check. I drank some more beer and avoided meeting anyone's eye.

Hot towels arrived; we all grabbed at them. I wiped one around my neck and across my face, over the top of my chest and through my sticky fingers, feeling the small ecstasy of its heat and then as it cooled, a return to normal. But nothing was normal as my eyes slowly refocused and I saw that everyone was staring at me.

Jack was gazing at me too, incredulous. 'I've never seen anyone do that with a chapatti.'

I had hoped to learn more about international cuisine through my many exotic trips, but in my twelve months at Roads Less Travelled the farthest I travelled was to the toilets on the third floor. Yet there was nowhere in the world I would rather have been. Out of Covent Garden station I came at a half-run each morning in my flowerpot hat, rucksack slung over one shoulder, laces undone, 'The Only Way Is Up' vibrating through body and brain.

I bought doughnuts for everyone in the office in the mornings and flirted and flitted my way through the working day, going up and down the stairs as often as I could – sometimes barefoot in my home from home – pretending to be up to my ears. There was always some vital fact to run by Jack, an opportunity for a well-rehearsed witty aside.

When I sensed a colleague nearing my desk, Chris or Jack in particular, I would tilt forwards in my chair, till I could see what was in front of me and scowl at my screen, brows contorted in concentration – pulling the sort of face you pull when you're at a gallery pretending to be profoundly interested in a piece of conceptual art you don't like or understand. When questions were directed at me I would deliberately not reply to create the impression of being so utterly absorbed in my work that I was unaware of anything having been said. I could sense people smile at the commitment of their bright new editorial assistant.

Privately, the sort of things I contemplated were what Jack was wearing on any particular day. If he wore a male version of what I'd worn to work the day before – a white T-shirt and a pair of jeans, for example – I thought it simply couldn't have been more obvious that he was interested in me. I cringed for him at times with the frequency of his visits to my desk under the pretence of concern for my work, at the deliberate adoption of my seat to illustrate something on my screen, the warmth of his backside left lingering.

If the account of Germany I was proofing was in any way tricky or dull, I would stride business-like through Editorial with *The Catcher in the Rye* under my arm, concealed in a brown envelope. Up in the third-floor toilets I'd read, paint my toenails cherry or listen to people chatting to each other from the cubicles on either side of me. Sometimes I'd join the smokers on the stairs. I smoked a cigarette once and found it erotic, like the first time I borrowed Pie's bra, but I preferred Nicorette gum. Carrie had been trying to give up and through peer pressure I'd become addicted.

In the evenings everyone went down to the Club – a community centre on Neal Street we shared with the local residents. While stiff old men lowered themselves into their particular seats for the night, alcoholic couples rowed over who was getting the next one in, children chased each other round the pool table or kicked their legs against bar stools, eating crisps, picking their noses, blowing bubbles through the straws of their fizzy drinks. There were events almost nightly – pub quizzes, pool tournaments, football matches screened on the TV above the fish tank, brawls, stolen bags, snatched kisses in the downstairs toilets that smelt of old women.

We all celebrated when Wimbledon beat Liverpool in the finals of the FA Cup. Down at the Club there were drinks on the house and a rousing performance from Roads Less Travelled's band. Closing time came and the fate of the night was decided in those fragile few minutes. Lights were switched on, the floating spell of the evening broken, chairs were hauled onto tables, the crowd coaxed out with the roars of the barmen. On the street, happiness hung on a knife-edge, as it does when you like someone: would Jack stay or go? Would he ask me to go with him? In those tense moments it could have gone either way. Jack could have been asked to share a cab home, he could have got impatient with the collective indecision about where to go, one of us could have been refused entry into a night bar.

Taxis were hailed, people ran for last Tubes and Jack stayed. Though it was still unspoken – to have mentioned it would have ruined everything – I basked in that deliciously thrilling moment of realization: I hadn't imagined it, he was interested in me and something was going to happen between us that night. There were niggles, as there always were: the jumper tucked into jeans, a goofy thing said, slightly cheesy breath, but I overlooked these, this was what I'd daydreamed about for months, pined for, and it becoming a reality was the best feeling in the world. I stepped out into the night, invincible.

Chris suggested we go back to the office – just the core group – Jack, Carrie and me – where he had a bottle of tequila, bought on a recent trip. We necked it between us, cross-legged on the floor in Chris's office, and spun the empty bottle round on the carpet. There we stayed for the night, four shrieking shadows up on the second floor, the spinning bottle glinting under the lamplights of Long Acre, as it slowed, stopped, was spun round again. Tops came off in truth or dare, warm wriggle-tongued kisses in ears. Hands, faces, mouths, near. Knickers were toyed with then tugged playfully down. Kisses, deeper now, and the hot rub of carpet on skin.

I was at my desk early the following morning, having slept in the pull-out bed of the caravan. Carrie and I went over to Gap to purchase new T-shirts to change into so no one would suspect we hadn't been home. I loved that staying up all night had given my voice a husky edge. I loved the impression I was building of being the sort of person who could stay out late and joke around the office all day but be so naturally competent that I could still get through my work.

When I tried to focus on the words on my screen they were blurred and dancing and meaningless to me. I had stored my contact lenses in a glass of water for the night and accidentally swallowed them some time before dawn. They were the first purchase I'd made with my First Direct credit card. Since my last test my sight had deteriorated significantly; I was now a minus seven in my good eye. They had been a disaster, I'd lost them, torn them, put them on inside out, and rather than making my eyes appear more attractive, the lenses dried them out and made them look red and tired. I tried to think of yeast. Sun rises in the east. Was that why men love making bread, I wondered, because of the yeast? Why men love to knead, because it's like fondling a woman's breasts? I wanted to rest my head, to sleep for a while, to think about the previous night's heat.

When deadlines slipped and questions started being asked, I told Chris that I was feeling a bit pressured, promising that if he could just ease off and be a little more encouraging with me, he would soon see results. I used to argue the same point with my father.

Privately I was panicking. The thought of trying to hold down a job I had no real understanding of, or interest in, was making me ill. Despite what I'd said at my interview and at every interview I'd ever had, I was hopeless under pressure. What I hadn't told my parents or anyone else was that since I'd got my job at Roads

Less Travelled I had dropped out of university. I had written and posted a letter to the head of the German department saying that I felt certain I had made the right decision – I was so fulfilled in my new job and had finally found my calling.

I was also bothered that Jack appeared to be avoiding me. Although he was still my mentor, the more mistakes I made, the less attention he paid me. As my position became more vulnerable, he became more distant until he began to ignore me entirely. This was more upsetting than the work I couldn't manage and I noticed, unimpressed with myself, just how much his behaviour was distracting me. The less encouraging he was the less motivated I became. He was doing exactly what my father did when he was disappointed with me.

I began enlisting anyone I knew in London or Dublin to help me. I started to work weekends, but all to no avail. Chris said that while I was great fun to have around the office, he had no option but to extend my probation period for the first time in Roads Less Travelled's history.

That year saw the launch of Prozac; newsreader Sue Lawley was attacked by lesbian protesters during her bulletin, the Turin Shroud was declared a fake, Salman Rushdie published his *Satanic Verses* to much controversy and I clung desperately to my job.

With circumstances in the office reaching crisis point and to distract from my incompetence I endeavoured to highlight my team-working skills by organizing an office away day in the shape of a Roads Less Travelled tennis tournament.

On a perfect late-summer afternoon: airbrushed sky, slanting shadows on sun-bleached streets – the sort of day that often made me lonely with the sense that everyone was having more fun than me, heading for the sea, driving off to the countryside for picnics – we made our way through Bloomsbury to the park in High Holborn, all twenty-five of us, bouncing balls on rackets, talking of partners and strategic game plans.

Relieved to find the courts I'd reserved unlocked and free when we got there – empty umpire chairs, nets dancing in the breeze – I unpacked the refreshments of orange and lemonade and sorted people out with their opponents.

It was to be a mixed-doubles event. Names were selected from a hat and I had been partnered with the head of accounts, Roger, who played for his local club and was keenly competitive. Soon colleagues who had never liked each other were running after balls and apologizing for poorly hit returns; the marketing manager's wife and children settled themselves on a picnic rug courtside. Even those who for some reason couldn't participate – Shane from marketing who had just the one leg, Joe who suffered from asthma and Kate, somewhat overweight – watched from the side-lines.

Having seen off the opposition, Roger and I made it to the finals where we met Carrie and Chris. Roger served for the match as I bounced about at the net, shooting glances back at him. He had the oddest, longest build-up to a serve – racket arm swishing about as if he were swatting flies, bum out, bum in, bum out again. Finally, with all the momentum of a catapult, he flung his racket at the ball. His serve landed in and as I squinted to place Chris's return hurtling through the sky – an easy volley – Regina Canning's face appeared.

Eyes straining to focus on the ball, I whacked my racket in its general direction and watched it travel beyond the baseline. 'Out!' the umpire shouted. But the match was not over. Roger took pretty much all of my shots after that and we went on to win the Roads Less Travelled tournament. Swelling with pride, we were hoisted on shoulders, hats were flung in the air. Congratulations and celebrations and down to the Club we all went, the end of a perfect day.

I came home late that night, and most nights of that year, if I came home at all, stumbling past the room where Patsy slept, clean-faced, unimpressed, over notes about overdue bills, notes that Mum had phoned, to the sitting-room where I ate processed cheese and crisps, flicking through TV channels, the spin cycle of Patsy's white wash upsetting the reception, club music ringing in my ears. Patsy and I hadn't seen much of each other lately. I was taken up with work and since she'd got a job as a Junior in a large Soho-based PR agency, she'd made a new set of friends who held dinner parties and went walking in the Lake District at weekends.

That year's Christmas party coincided with my twentieth birthday and the termination of my twelve-month probation at Roads Less Travelled. The stereo throbbed through the office that afternoon. Work was winding down, the holidays were near and everyone was taking it easy.

I wish I'd seen Jack approaching my desk; I'd been whining along to 'Fairytale of New York', swaying my head, showing off that I knew all the words and what I considered the uncanny resemblance my voice bore to Kirsty MacColl's. He asked if we could have a quick chat. I gave him a flirty grin – relieved that whatever had been bothering him had passed and that he was talking to me again – grabbed a packet of Nicorette gum and followed him into the caravan. We sat down together on the bench seat, knee touching knee, an Armani arm stretched protectively behind me. He asked me how I thought I was getting along, delivering the question to my left breast, I observed with a private smile (he had a sort of facial tic that made him address me like this). I told him that I still found the whole north/west thing a little tricky, but aside from that everything was dandy. I simply couldn't have been enjoying myself more. I felt I was learning and contributing.

Chris came in to join us. With his head at a tilt and an expression of weary exasperation washing over his face, he told me that he thought I should leave. He'd run out of ideas; it just wasn't working out. I was stunned, speechless. I locked my eyes on my frantically fidgeting hands and held them there. My throat had tightened so much it was difficult to swallow; I made audible gulping sounds. They had said all there was to say and were awaiting my response. How could I salvage this?

I lifted my head to the light of the window, unable to bring myself to look at either Chris or Jack and promised to try harder, to get in earlier, tried once more to convince them that I was right for the job, made excuses, blamed other people, agreed that I had become a little too distracted by the social element, and vowed that I would go to the Club less often and be on time for meetings. I got angry, got defensive and when none of this worked, I cried. My skin prickled as I watched the rest of the office through the caravan window: normal, functioning, intelligent human beings, concentrating, getting along with their lives, getting their work done. This was the place where I felt I belonged and now I was being rejected from. I felt I might be sick. How could this be happening? I thought everyone liked me.

I excused myself and climbed the stairs to the toilets on the third floor, legs buckling, head throbbing, and locked myself in a cubicle, shredding toilet tissue with my fingers as I sobbed.

An e-mail had already been circulated to the rest of staff by the time I'd returned to my desk, saying that I had taken the decision to leave, a decision that might have been more believable if I hadn't looked suicidal.

The phone rang. It was Mum just wanting to wish me a happy birthday. There was nothing more certain to make me fall apart than hearing my mother's buoyed-up voice from over the Irish Sea. My eyes were hot. I knew the tears would start again if I tried to tell her what had happened so I said something about an important meeting and put the phone down.

I shoved through the swing doors and down the stairs, without jacket or bag, and battled through the Covent Garden afternoon of Christmas lights and cheer, bawling freely. I didn't care who saw. This was worse than any break-up – I wasn't only losing a job, I was losing my foster family.

The park in High Holborn was empty. It wasn't an afternoon for the park unless you were snuggled up with your boyfriend, drinking hot chocolate from the same cup. The nets had been removed from the tennis courts and were wrapped up under the umpire's chair.

I thought someone from the office might have run after me – Carrie or Jack maybe. It felt clichéd to be crumpled up on a park bench crying, as though someone had just shouted Action and I was told to play the part of a lost soul; but there was no one watching, no one to hear or see me.

And as I sat there, I became aware of another feeling competing with despair: relief, a tidal wave of it. I had bluffed my way into a job that I not only had no aptitude for, but that was everything I hated: fact checking, timetables, opening hours, rules, confinement, rigidity. Adhering to a style guide and fussing over details in the small print had bored me rigid. I didn't want to create books for other people's enjoyment, I wanted to add colour to the passages, to include my own observations to places I'd never seen but had imagined daily, vividly.

The traffic grumbled on under an endless porridge sky. How I hated to think about the sky being endless.

'Birthday girl! Party girl! Atta girl!' roared Tyrone, lead singer of Roads Less Travelled's band, as he bounced and strummed the opening bars of 'Lucy in the Sky with Diamonds' at the Christmas party that night. Carrie had eventually hunted me down at the park, made up my face in a hotel toilet, taken me to a nearby pub, plied me with vodka and cajoled me into coming to the party. Two hundred writers, staff and guests, clapped and laughed at the surprise they had given me for my birthday. With all those heads turned in my direction, I tried to laugh along. As soon as I could I pulled some guy from the party – Simon, I think he was; floppy-haired, sweet, I knew he liked me.

Over Waterloo Bridge we went piggyback, down to the river, shrieking, giddy, to dangle our feet in the Thames. He spun me upside down on the sand: silver buildings shimmering in water, the dank underbelly of the bridge, a different view of the London night racing by, so vast, so lonely.

I let them stare at us kiss pressed up against the wall, let them pass and go, nothing mattered but me and him and the rush through the tunnel of warm Tube air, blowing voices, blowing hair, approaching train, all aboard. We sat opposite each other like strangers, pulling cross faces, cross-eyes, blowing kisses and sticking out tongues. I read over the over-coated shoulder of the man beside me. Sober, alone, on his way home, he didn't have what we had that night.

Linking arms we stumbled through the dark alleyway at the end of Berwick Street, by the shuttered windows of Nice to Meat You butchers, past haberdashery and rag trade shops. Forlorn during the day, at night this alleyway became a mini-acropolis of sin: flashing neon-lit peep shows, *Nude Nudes*, lap dancing clubs behind quiz-show tinsel streamers, dirty book shops and free-lancing prostitutes, tired women in satin dresses, short men in suits, beckoning. We pondered a corner shop that had a colourful display of stacked and rampant 'Rabbits' in its window, reminding me of old Mrs Grimshaw and her early torch-like model, the 'Non Doctor'. Vaguely disgusted and at the same time fascinated by the sort of person who frequented such places, I peered through the half-tinted windows, drink, darkness and Simon's company making me bold.

Flicking through a magazine at the back section of the shop was a young man who looked perfectly normal, not unlike my older brother, Ollie, in fact, with his lanky, hand-in-pocket stance. He turned his face sideways to call his friend over and I realized in an instant and with a thrill that it *was* Ollie! What was he doing here, in London? Why hadn't he contacted me? Pointing him out to Simon excitedly, I rapped my fist against the window, like a child at an aquarium, and shouted his name. I wanted to see him; he would help me out, save me, Ollie always made things better. Simon put his hand over my mouth, abruptly shutting me up, and suggesting, with bewilderingly sudden sobriety that the last person my brother would want to meet in a porn palace would be his baby sister. Couldn't I see that there was something wrong with the picture?

I was drunkenly insistent that we hang about in the area, perhaps some distance from the shop, and wait for Ollie to appear, at which point I would pretend to accidentally bump into him, ignoring, of course, any paper bag or parcel under his arm.

The spitting sleet added to Simon's argument; we took shelter in the doorway of a nearby upmarket restaurant and joked about getting a table. I was still adamant that I wanted to wait for Ollie, but Simon encouraged me indoors.

They sat us at a window seat of upholstered green leather and blindingly white table linen, and fussed over us as though we had money. Simon attempted to reassure me as my humour vacillated between hysteria and maudlin gloom. Left alone – where did Simon say he was going? – I watched, through stained-glass windows, the shifting shadows of passing pedestrians under umbrellas.

On a wood-panelled wall opposite me were portraits of famous literary faces: Robert Burns, Philip Larkin, Samuel Beckett. Playing with candle wax I studied them. Printed on plaques beneath each were the jobs they had done before they achieved success: Customs and Excise Officer, Assistant Librarian, an Orderly at a mental asylum.

I had to distract myself; I was afraid to let myself think; life had become too confusing. There was still no sign of Ollie – nothing was as it seemed.

11

Excess baggage

It was my last day in London. In those first few minutes of luxurious half-sleep there was calm, serenity. My thoughts were soothing – firelight, Mum's enveloping hugs, the warmth of risen radiators, the shipping forecast on the kitchen radio, from Malin Head to Mizen Head, bath water, toast and tea.

Children were shrieking like seagulls in the playground, wherever the playground was – somewhere behind the house, beyond the tight network of gardens, sheds, fences, rooftops, trees – taunting me with all the time I'd lost listening to their races and games in my bed of crumbs and pillows heavy with the smell of my head, too hung-over or too lazy to get up. I wished I could begin again like them, with careful handwriting on the first page of a new copybook, with my full name embroidered into my school uniform.

I was leaving all of this for good. The oddly high door handles, the pencil-drawn Indians above the cupboard with the ironing board. The particular cast of a morning shadow on the bedroom ceiling, which turned the lamp and its chains into an eyeball stretched from its socket as if in shock, held only by straining tendons and threads.

Sound seemed clearer that last day somehow, the drone of traffic closer, the wood pigeon's cooing acute, water gurgling through pipes, my feet heavy on a colder floor: the soundtrack of me leaving. I dragged my bags through the hall, past the bike of the man upstairs I had never seen. Maybe I was right to be leaving a city where people could live behind the same front door for a year and never once meet.

The endless openings and closings of the front door hadn't cleared the hall of its wet-ashtray smell. Uncollected post lay on the white table that was missing a caster. I held them close for scrutiny: an electricity bill addressed to a Mr Sakkas, an envelope informing Victoria Enright that she was *Reader's Digest*'s thousandth winner, a court summons with my name on it, for non-payment of Council Tax – they'd never find me now.

Patsy had been headhunted to run an art gallery in Dublin – I was travelling home alone. This made me nervous – I'd become uneasy about venturing anywhere that I wasn't physically familiar with. Over our years in London my relationship with Patsy had changed. Because I couldn't see what I was doing anymore, I'd had to relinquish control. It became incumbent on Patsy to check train timetables, to hold her hand out for buses. She strode ahead of me into pubs to locate friends; she got our orders in at Burger King because I could no longer read the board.

I'd worked it out wrong. I had too much stuff and no easy way of getting to the airport: bags and bundles, bedding, posters and postcards, and always one more thing. What I needed was the luxury of a taxi: all door to door and happy chat along the way, but since I'd lost my job and First Direct had closed my account and ordered me to cut up my credit card, the Tube was the only option available.

With bedding eclipsing my face and holdall heavy on my shoulder, I pulled the front door behind me and plodded down Mansfield Road. No one saw me go, or if they did, they didn't say anything. Only a dog behind a gate sensed an encroachment, yelping as I passed.

On the street I felt conspicuous. Where before I was a shadow, unworthy of comment, today I was suspicious, stealing away with my bags of booty and tat. Like a prostitute caught in bright daylight – all wrong and out of place and time, dislodged from my doorway and dishevelled in the public stare.

A jogger bounded off the pavement and onto the road to run around me, turning into Hampstead Heath at the entrance by the Lido. The Heath, which would forever hold the promise of boisterous picnics with friends, of warm Sunday paper snoozes and sleepy deep sex in the meadow grass, giddy heads throbbing with boldness and longing. Of substantial walks in October's clear air, days of kite flying on Parliament Hill with children and their sticky hands, and piggy-back rides home for tea.

These were days that rarely happened and on the odd occasions that they did, never lived up to the excitement of their imaginings. But their possibility alone made them something worth missing, when that possibility was removed. Now that they would never happen, those days were something to miss.

The Odeon was showing *Rain Man*. It was showing it that Saturday night when the ticket machine jammed and a father crumpled up with a heart attack. Cinemagoers stepped around him, over him, with their credit cards and quarrels, as a daughter and a mother stood falling apart and an ambulance man from the Royal Free tried and failed to restart his system.

I stood still on the escalator to the underground, too lethargic to walk, and imagined sliding down the steel central section. I often contemplated doing this for fun or for a dare, but that morning I imagined flinging myself down, being buffeted against steel. Whack, tumble, crack, smack, fall.

Peering over the platform edge, I tried to frighten myself. Mice skittered up and down along the greased tracks – how boring it must be to be an underground mouse, to have to run for cover every two minutes of your life. And how strange to be a Tube driver, a stroboscopic life, charging over those mice, snaking from dark to light all day in an airless grey shell, more cautious perhaps on the feast of Saint Valentine, when some lonely soul might fling themselves in front of you.

I had refused to say goodbye to any of my colleagues at Roads Less Travelled because I didn't want to accept that I wasn't coming back. On my desk I had left a couple of possessions exactly as they were: my grey hooded cardigan on the back of my chair, my Roads Less Travelled tennis trophy on the windowsill. I felt certain I'd return. Not in my former capacity perhaps, but in some new, tailor-made role – a General Office Assistant maybe, a handy sort of person to have around the building, to fix things, to prepare sandwiches for meetings, to pop out to the post office in the afternoons. I met Carrie for lunch a few days after I'd been told to leave. She had my cardigan and tennis trophy in a box.

It seemed wrong to be jetting home when I'd made such a huge mess of everything. I should have been on the boat-train via Crewe. Paddy goes to Holyhead. The great expectations and subsequent fall made me think of the occasion of our school centenary Mass. I and five other specially selected singers stood at the altar in front of an expectant congregation waiting for Mrs French, poised at the organ in the gallery, to provide us with the opening chord for 'Through the Darkness Shining'. She began two keys too high, her mouth forming an exaggerated O to act as a prompt for us. We strained to reach it then broke into convulsive giggles.

Through muffled hysteria and missed notes, Patsy and I, too silly and giddy to pull ourselves together as the others had done, botched all eight of the hymns we performed that day, perspiration heavy in our armpits, sudden bursts from our noses rubbed away with sleeves or sniffed back up from whence they came. At the end of each hymn we tottered off the altar, single file as rehearsed, and retook our seats in a satisfied way, music sheets resting on knees. There we would feel the prod in our backs of the fat finger of our Religion teacher, sitting tweed-suited in the pew behind us, livid and spitting threats in our ears.

An empty Coke bottle rolled around the carriage floor as the train rattled and sped, a page three girl pouted on the seat beside me from a discarded copy of the *Sun*. At each station new people carried new smells on, merging with old smells left behind. There was nothing more redolent of the underground than its smells: the fuming funnel of tunnel air, the sharp saltiness of an armpit in the rush-hour crush, the carrot-soup sick of the platform-booted punk who got on at Camden and spewed till she staggered off at Tufnell Park, the lemon-clean woman beside her who rummaged for a hanky to help. The sweet stuffiness of Mum's perfumed hair on our way to the theatre when she came over to visit me that weekend.

Our train stopped at Hammersmith. An elderly man hoisted himself up opposite me and began a painstaking shuffle towards the door, nose almost meeting knees, he was so folded over. He looked like Pinocchio's Geppetto – trousers held high with braces, a white work shirt under an elbow-patched cardigan, a ring of snow round his small brown head. He had twisted the handles of a plastic bag through the yellowed fingers of his left hand, as knobbled and lean as bamboo shoots. His free arm swung from its socket as though it were treading water.

With one foot safely on the platform, he was steadying himself and was about to address the matter of the other, when the bleeping began and the train doors moved to close. He cleared his leg and his hand in time, but his plastic bag got caught in the sliding doors. As the train pulled away, the man held fast, slapping his loose-hinged feet against the platform tiles as he moved. I stood up to help, as did another passenger, but neither of us knew what to do. When the train picked up speed he let go. The doors opened at the next station. Inside the carriage the bag fell to the floor. Out rolled a parsnip, across the ridges, spinning and travelling on alone.

Still standing, I stared vacantly at the advertisements on the carriage wall.

I dropped two dress sizes in a week with Slimfast Supershakes!

Eye Laser surgery changed my life. I found a new job, a new relationship ... everything changed because I could see clearly.

Get a free large fries with every Big Mac Meal!

Underneath this advert a note in small print read:

This offer is not available to people who live in Berkhampstead.

Eye Laser surgery changed my life.

I dully eyed the route we were taking – Acton, Northfields, Boston Manor – places I would only ever get a back-garden glimpse of. An endless flicker of ever-changing slides: life was changing, altering again, delivering me away from all that was happily established.

The train charged from dark into light, slapping through tunnels, lurching round corners, straightening and expanding out into the smoky suburban haze. Where was I off to in such a hurry? To lie on the bench in the kitchen like a teenager on an endless summer holiday, bored and picking at the glue on the table's underside, with a knee-down view of the world. Pie in odd socks, her shuffle from kettle to cupboard and back to kettle again, clearing her throat as she does without needing to. Mum's uncrossed legs under the table, slightly apart and absolutely still as if she thinks she's heard something and is waiting to hear it again, both of them gabbling and interrupting each other's sentences.

I was going home to drag around the supermarket beside Mum's trolley till someone could come up with something useful to do with me. Maybe I'd make myself busy having a breakdown, something with a name for it, a way to behave, an excuse to opt out. Leave her alone, they'd say. Let her lie in bed rocking with the curtains closed if she wants. That's what broken people do. Poor old Bunty Boo, she's just a little confused. They'd have to wheelchair me into Dublin Airport, tired, floppy, failed and deliver me home to be cuddled and spoon-fed.

And yet I had a growing sense that all of this had

been inevitable, that I was never going to fit into the nine to five; that I was destined for something else. What that something else was, I wasn't sure yet, but I thought I might experiment with something creative, the way my father had wanted to write poetry. I thought of the letter I'd found. I wanted to read it again. I should have taken it with me when we left the cottage in Hampstead.

Through the carriage window opposite, my reflection appeared blurred and grainy like those out-of-focus photos in newspapers in memory of the dead. At the family Christmas party I would have to be handled with care. There would be corner whispers with my parents by the drinks cabinet. No, it hadn't worked out. No money made, no invaluable experience gained, no excellent references, no promotions, no weight lost, no new hair, no *Doesn't Lucy look well!*

Osterley, Hounslow West, Hatton Cross. Old telegraph poles, a closed sofa factory, rush-hour starlings swooping home to their broods.

When my ticket wouldn't let me through the barriers at the airport, a woman from London Underground with the 'No' sort of face you find in a bank jerked her head in the direction of the Excess Fares window while cleaning the underside of a star-spangled thumbnail between her bottom front teeth.

Once I'd checked in I sank down on my duvet and waited for my gate to be announced. The panicked surge of a world on the move pushed and fussed around me in a frenzy of last-called flights, lost children, confusions of colour, confusions of lights. Happy people going home to families who were proud of them with Christmas presents bought and jobs to return to. Clear-headed, organized people filling in their luggage tags and fragile bags and diaries of plans made and money saved – and then me. Curled up in the corner like any old tramp in any old city, a lost detail in a Richard Scarry sketch.

I sat in my window seat as lightly as I could, the extra luggage I'd snuck on and the exceptionally large lady lowering herself into a seat in front of mine making me worry that we were listing. I watched the shivering streams of sleet through the corner of my plastic port-hole as we taxied down the runway. I hated flying. I pictured planes like jet fighters duck-diving to dodge each other in the sky. I hated the pilot chatting to reassure us, I didn't want to be warned about possible turbulence or engine trouble or bombs on board, I wanted him to concentrate, to keep his eyes on the sky. I rated the potential of a pilot by the way he spoke – a British accent was my favourite, an American next, a female voice was alarming. I studied the expressions of the air hostesses – why would anyone do this job? I would rather eat bees than push a trolley through a steel tube thirty thousand feet up.

Nose pressed against the window as we came in to land; the misery of Christmas ahead. How could I tell my parents that another job had gone? I was still trying to figure out how to tell them I'd dropped out of university. What would my father say – if he could bring himself to say anything at all? He had seemed proud of me for the first time when I'd got my job at Roads Less Travelled; now he would revert to his default position, bitter disappointment. I wondered what I'd done with that travel book he'd sent. I wanted to look at it again; I'd begun reading it lately and liked the way the words were expressed. There was an old charm and careful attention to the choice of phrase, eloquence that seemed lacking in what I had been accustomed to in the office. There was a generosity in its descriptions and a beguiling sense of adventure. He had sent me that book because it was well written and in a style that perhaps I could have aspired to.

Presents from my father were always educational, except for that one Christmas when he bought Pie and me a shirt each: blue for me because of my eyes, a red one for Pie. They were from A-Wear and were fashionable at the time – long-sleeved and boyish with buttons and small collars and longer tail bits at the back.

It was impossible to visualize my father in a women's clothes shop – to imagine him flicking through the rails, comparing textures and styles, with modern music assaulting his ears. How did he know our sizes? How much he might have to pay? Each shirt was carefully gift-wrapped, presumably a seasonal service provided by the shop, but the paper he'd chosen was in our colours too, so there wouldn't be any confusion. I remember him standing in the hall as we opened the parcels on Christmas Day, not knowing what to do with his hands, finally joining them together behind his back, waiting to see what we thought.

I can't remember ever wearing mine, but I did yank it from the cupboard and fling it at him during a fight. His head jerked back and his hand shot up to his glasses in reflex, unsure of what was being thrown. I yelled that I hated the colour, that I'd never wear it, that he probably hadn't even bothered to choose it for me, that he must have got Mum to buy it, that I hated everything about it, that I hated him. Then I took a great swing at my bedroom door.

There was no sleet in Dublin that night, it was just grey old kitchen-sink wet. The 'F' in the huge neon-lit 'Fáilte' sign suspended from the ceiling at Arrivals in Dublin Airport was dangling upside down like a back-to-front t. Swinging from a single nail, it fizzed weakly.

The city seemed squat and rural as it always did on that first journey from the airport through eyes accustomed to the imposing buildings of London. But it was home and safe and unquestioning and I knew I would adjust to it in time.

I told Mum I'd take the bus. Dazed with tiredness, I got out at Donnybrook Garage and walked the few hundred yards home, hoping everyone was asleep.

The front drive was empty of cars apart from our own. The bare arms of the oak tree were reflected in the night-blackened windows of the dining-room and no one appeared to be up. I closed the front door extra gently. Taking off my runners and holding one in each hand, I padded my way confidently through the hall – night vision was day vision for me – past the grandfather clock stretched ghostly long in the dark and up the stairs to my room.

Mum heard me. She was sitting up in bed with a squished pillow behind her. Beside her bedside lamp was a book-marked thriller that she must have just put down. She was in her nightdress – a *Little House on the Prairie* style white one with frills along the cuffs and the bust line – but she'd tied a russet-coloured scarf round her neck and was fully made-up.

She'd had her Colour Me Beautiful colours done that afternoon. Through stiff lips and with her chin held artificially high so nothing would shift or smudge, she said she'd wanted to keep the make-up on to show me when I got home. She was a spring–autumn combination she said, lowering her lids to reveal splodges of caramel-coloured cream around their creases, twisting her face this way and that to display the bold sweeps of blusher across her cheekbones, and puckering up her plum lips which looked disconcertingly sexy.

We chatted about my terrible trip and what we might do the next day. She had made up my old room and put a hot-water bottle between the sheets so it would be nice and warm. My father was asleep in the spare room, where he often went to avoid her snores. She looked at me as if she knew something was wrong, but also to say that she didn't want to know. For my mother bad news was something to be hummed through and ignored. I presented my forehead to kiss; I'd tell her about my uncertain future in the morning. She said something else once I'd closed the door, the way she always does when she's just out of earshot.

12

Standard bog day

In the months following an un-heroic return to Dublin, my position in a hazy world became ever more nebulous. I seemed to be fading, disappearing from view, like the little boy in *The Shrinking of Treehorn* who had grown so small by the end of the book that he could walk underneath his own bed.

I was an oddity in a city I no longer knew, skulking through streets, plunging into puddles I couldn't see, having dances with strangers, stepping to the left, stepping to the right, apologizing, bumping into them, pushing pull doors, nearly getting knocked down, smiling at neighbours who didn't smile back.

Even Mum had to double-check my identity. She'd volunteered to take the electoral register for our constituency during the local elections and was unusually laconic when I arrived at the polling station to vote. She dragged her ruler down the page of registered voters in the area, not once, but twice to look for my name, before asking officiously if she could see some form of ID. I played along, assuming that she was being aloof in order to appear professional to her fellow register checkers. It only occurred to me as I left that perhaps she had wanted to create a little distance between herself and her troubled, underachieving daughter.

Without ever having discussed it, my father and I had devised ways of avoiding each other while living at the same address. He was often away with work, his most recent successes taking him on lengthy trips to the continent, often for weeks at a time, and when he was at home we ate, slept and watched television in different rooms and at different times of the day. It wasn't unlike the relationship I'd had with the man in London who lived upstairs. He took up more or less permanent residency in his study – reading, working, writing, thinking, doing, finishing – while Mum delivered and collected his meals on a tray. I stayed in my room where I listened out for the twist of the key in the study door, whereupon I would venture downstairs. After a lifetime of avoiding him, I had begun to time things so that I would bump into my father and attempt to strike up a conversation. But he was too exhausted with me to communicate; he'd done ten rounds and needed time to recover his strength. My mother encouraged this distance between us as being beneficial to his health.

If we encountered each other on the street and happened to be walking in the same direction, we would walk along together to begin with, the way related people do, or rather he would walk and I would trot beside him to keep up with his stride, which seemed to lengthen when I joined him. I'd ask him what he was up to and where he was going and he would answer me, but he didn't enquire about what I was doing or where I was going in return.

He didn't say I was made-up like a dog's dinner any more and he had given up correcting my pronunciation and posture. He would come up with an excuse to part when we inevitably ran out of conversation – to turn back for a forgotten thing, to move ahead in a hurry. We were a father and his daughter but out of the context of home we were two individuals with nothing to say to each other; two strangers who just happened to be walking along the same street.

I was keen to talk to him about the letter to his mother, about his poetry – would he mind if I read some of it? – to tell him about some of the ideas I had had for short stories. More than anything I wanted to ask him about this side to him I had never seen. It was odd to think of my father as a man, as another human being, as someone entirely separate from me. There's an old photograph of him before he was my father at all, sitting in faded wine-coloured togs on a rock, the sea behind him, his arms curled around his knees. It's badly taken, one of his ears is missing as is an elbow and half a left leg, and behind his glasses his eyes are closed against the glare of the flash, perhaps, or with the harshness of the sun. There may have been someone beside him, maybe to the left of him just out of view, but the warmth of his smile isn't for that person, it's for the face behind the camera, the anonymous photographer's squinting eye. Was he the same man or was he someone different, happier, more himself?

I was lying on the bench in the kitchen pondering my hair colour and what it was that I was meant to be one Monday morning, when Mum came in carrying the remains of the kippers my father had eaten for breakfast. (On the first day of their marriage my father had brought my mother breakfast in bed; on the second day my mother did the same for my father. They both seemed more comfortable with the latter arrangement so they'd been doing it that way ever since.) She was ebullient with the news that a position had been found for me in the Civil Service. I didn't want a position in the Civil Service. Mum pointed out that as it had taken all my father's influence to secure, I would jolly well have to accept it.

It was a lowly, unchallenging post without the bonus of a coat-stand or car park space to which more senior servants were privileged. An uncomplicated job that my father prayed I would manage without causing him further embarrassment. At the very least I wouldn't be making a nuisance of myself at home any more. I would be out from under everyone's feet.

Most people take lifts to go up – up to airy offices, to space, colour and light cascading through windows and monitors and overhead reading lamps – to team-build and brainstorm and power-nap and practise yoga and network and personally advance.

My journey didn't take me up. I waited to descend, with the janitor's trolley, cardboard boxes for recycling and leaking bin bags, to an airless, windowless dungeon. There I joined other troglodytes – the long-term temps, the travellers, the dodgers, the drifters, the lost, the lazy, the young – to lick and staple and stuff.

Dolores was at her desk already when I arrived, the first competition of the day won. She was in before me, which automatically proved that she was a harder worker. I was the first person Dolores had ever been in charge of. For fifteen years she'd been taking orders from others and there was nothing that gave her more satisfaction than to exercise the small amount of power she had over me.

When Dolores spoke she spoke in platitudes but when they came out of her mouth they came out upside down, the wrong way round, or entirely reinvented. 'I just wish they'd let us know nay or hay,' she said about something or other as Maura breezed in all fluttery freshness and seizing the day, carrying a cake-shaped surprise wrapped in tinfoil, murmuring positive affirmations and smelling like a Carefree panty pad.

Maura was beyond retirement age but had carried on working because she enjoyed it, because she felt she was making a positive contribution to society. When she wasn't in Easons purchasing Mass cards, she was down at Glasnevin putting lilies on graves, one hand fiddling with the cross on her chest as she took a moment to remember her endless deceased relatives and friends. She was the sort of person who looked forward to taking down Christmas decorations.

Under the low-ceiling glare of a factory light peppered

with dead flies, in the fug of filing cabinets and books curling on shelves, I unpacked the tools of my trade from the shoebox in which they were contained: a large tub of glue, a pair of scissors, Sellotape and a paintbrush.

It was Dolores's job to go through the daily newspapers putting asterisks beside what she considered relevant stories and images for filing. These she passed on to me. It was up to me to cut and paste everything marked onto A4 sheets of paper and to sort them by subject and date.

My job wasn't a challenging one and generally it caused me no problems until I felt Dolores's beady eye on me, whereupon I would glue my thumbs together, unstick tape from one hand only for it to get stuck on the other, push my glasses back up my nose and affix my fingers to the frame. My latest pair were tortoiseshell framed, serious spectacles to match the severity of my disability, their black case with velvet lining a miniature coffin, befitting for my weakening vision now in its death throes. I peered out at the world through an opaque goldfish bowl.

From the corridor outside I could hear the torpid shuffle of the woman who worked in the post room – Eileen, or was it Irene? Swish swash swish swash, the tops of her polyester-clad thighs rubbed as she heaved boxes back and forth against her chest. Not really a chest when I thought about it – bosom was a more correct word for it. She had the sort of bust that probably started off as two separate breasts but had become, over the years, a solid singular bosom. She'd been trapped downstairs even longer than Dolores – seventeen years I think; her skin was almost translucent, so starved was it of natural light.

The telephone rang. In her capacity as receptionist the answering of telephones formed a fundamental part of her job, but Catherine let it carry on ringing, twice, three times, only leaning across her desk to pick it up with a resentful exhale on the fourth.

Unable to summon the energy to lift her tongue to the roof of her mouth to include the h of her name, she kept it where it was and dragged the letters through her teeth instead. 'Catrinn,' she droned into the mouthpiece. There was no one there after all that expended energy, just the flat-line screech of someone trying to send a fax through the phone.

It was unusual to see Catherine sitting at her desk; she was generally underneath it or not there at all. Being four months pregnant she rarely felt well enough to come to work and on the occasional days she made it in, she would announce soon afterwards that she was in no fit condition to be manning the phones. She lay instead on the floor beneath her desk massaging her stomach and inhaling deeply. She was under doctor's orders to eat every two hours. This helped with the nausea she complained of but resulted in terrible heartburn: coffee slices and cream buns repeating all over us whenever she felt well enough to speak.

The photocopier churned, jammed, stopped. Dolores turned a page of the newspaper, I sucked on a paper cut, tink tink from a teaspoon as Catherine stirred. Maura would see to it. Brushing imaginary crumbs off her cardigan, she ballet-stepped over to the machine to investigate.

On a shelf behind the photocopier was a spider plant, another day closer to death. Its parched leaves pleaded out of an old plastic pot. A brusque little woman came in once a week with a watering can, face set and powder-puffed under a helmet of silver hair, to attend to the aspidistra she'd rented to the office, but the spider plant was beyond her remit. No one could be bothered to do anything with it so there it hung expiring on the shelf, no food, no water, no light.

The hum of the humdrum: e-mails arriving, another letter sucked through the franking machine, the wonky-wheeled trolley along the corridor, the click of buttons on a Dictaphone, the tumble of fingers over keys. Sounds so unstimulating they only resonate once they've ceased.

Dolores's stapler was missing. She announced that she'd lost it, but I could tell from her tone and the way her eyes swivelled across my desk that she suspected it had been stolen rather than simply mislaid. I asked her what it looked like as I decapitated some government minister with the poorly judged positioning of my scissors. 'It's a standard bog one,' she said, 'Just a bog one,' with her name written across its base in Tippex.

The pond life ventured upstairs at eleven each morning for coffee break, our eyes adjusting to the natural light. Often everyone would assemble in a great fuss of extra chairs and of making room and once we'd sorted ourselves out and were sitting, no one could think of anything to say. Someone might bring up a salient point of news – 'Did you hear that women have started swimming in the Forty Foot in Sandycove?' – some had heard, some had not, but no one would have anything to add on the matter, and we'd all fall silent again. There we would sit for tortured minutes, clearing throats, intensely examining rag-nails.

It was during those long coffee breaks that I missed Roads Less Travelled most. I wondered what I'd have been doing if I'd still been there. Probably chilling out on the stairs with Carrie, tapping my feet to the moan of the blues. The smokers might be talking about Cambodia, the night before at the Club, the search for someone to cover the Roads Less Travelled to Rome. That someone would never be me, but the suggestion alone was exciting. Jack might sneak a wink at me; I'd return a hot-faced smile. Perhaps there'd be a surprise visit from an ex-member of staff, now resident in Cancun, with her beautiful raven-haired child.

The slicing of Maura's chocolate fudge cake made everyone smile, the way the prospect of cake or any type of dessert always does. Dolores disappeared into the kitchen to get some extra forks, a Post-it note stuck to her bum. The cake had been made for one of the temps, Miriam, who was due to leave that day for a better, long-term job in another department. An e-mail from Human Resources marked urgent had been sent around the office just prior to coffee break to say that due to some sort of mix-up Miriam's new job had fallen through. Naturally she was very upset, so we were all invited upstairs to offer our condolences and moral support. Maura dug her knife into the cake and doled out slices to everyone, giving Miriam the first. Forced to sit forward in her chair because Catherine's hefty arm was curled supportively around her shoulders, she nibbled at the icing like a hamster, the presence of the cake and the concern of her colleagues causing her eyes to brim with fresh tears.

Senior civil servants occasionally joined us for coffee break, at which point our stilted conversations would dry up altogether. Otherwise the only interaction we had with them was when we had to pass each other in the corridor. We might spot them from the middle distance but pretend that we hadn't to avoid the awkwardness of having to look at them when they were too far away to speak. As they neared us we would wet our lips in preparation, forgetting for a moment that they had no intention whatsoever of acknowledging us. In the Civil Service, unless you're at least a Higher Executive Officer, or your father is someone important, you shouldn't expect a hello.

Cormac was an exception. Cormac was the office joker; with his womanly thighs, flabby bottom, belt under belly, he was fat and funny and everyone's friend. Someone had told him once that he was funny and he'd been being funny ever since. He had a reason to talk to me that day. Dolores had volunteered me to help him set up for a conference in Limerick the following morning and we had travel arrangements to discuss. He finished, as he always did, with a joke. I hate being told jokes. I hate having to concentrate until the punchline and even then I never get them. I hate having to think of witty retorts. 'Boom Boom Tsch!' was how they always ended, Cormac moonwalking backwards out of the room, with an unsettling grin, top and bottom teeth bared, like the grille from a 1950s Oldsmobile.

I had a training session on how to use our new photocopier that afternoon. A man from Xerox had fanned his dimpled fingers on the table – their clammy imprint evaporating on the wood – and was midway through announcing that with the Xerox Super Delux 800 paper jams would be a thing of the past, when Dolores popped her head round the door. I stretched my arms over my notebook to conceal the character description I'd been writing of him. She ducked a futile few inches under the projector on her way over to me and whispered out loud that there had been a major 'foopon'.

I had known the faux pas would be spotted eventually; Dolores had probably waited until I was in a meeting to say anything about it. She liked to interrupt my meetings; she didn't want me getting above myself.

In the minister's foreword to our latest report, which Dolores had typed up and I had volunteered to proofread given my experience – Mum encouraged me to grab any chances like these for advancement – he had referred to 'the importance of improving our *pubic* services'; not just once, he'd repeated it three times for emphasis, the way all good politicians do. I had only noticed this typo after two thousand copies had been published and had prayed that no one else would.

Evening dragged in with the cleaner's black bag, the day almost at an end. Bins were emptied for the following day when it would all begin again. How and ever and in fairness, as they say in the Civil Service, it was a job, it was secure, there was a pension, and days off for shopping at Christmas.

13

Limerick junction
platform 2, waiting for a train

'Boom Boom Tsch!' Cormac's spit landed on my lip. Using his squat forefingers as drumsticks he bashed an imaginary cymbal and holding up his trouser legs to reveal a tantalizing glance of Manchester United socks, he flapped his feet in a little tap dance.

The sky was that suicide grey of a pebble-dash wall. No sun, no wind, no rain.

No train was coming. Grass grew over a rusted track. An old diesel engine had long given up. A supermarket trolley lay on its side, immobilized. The buckled wheel from a bicycle, 'Free Nicky Kelly', an abandoned left shoe.

The clock on the platform flicked.

'I have a great one for you ...' he said, moving to within kissing distance, egg and onion exhaling warmly over my face. I smiled with all the choice of a skull baring its teeth, left my exterior where it was and retreated like a hermit crab, two hollows where my eyes used to be.

An announcement was made on the station's speakers, but what came out was just a garbled vibrating noise and with Cormac's voice raised to make itself audible, the only decipherable words were an efficiently intoned 'thank you'.

A bluebottle landed on the shoulder of his suit. Cormac was oblivious; he had that smiling, staring off into the distance expression of someone searching their head for another good joke to tell.

'Boom Boom Tsch!'

I flapped the back of my hand in the direction of his shoulder. The fly didn't budge. It was frozen, feeding on the moist flakes of scalp skin from his oleaginous head and the bits of breakfast still lingering on his lapels.

No train was coming.

14

Missing

I pictured our house like a doll's house that Thursday evening; each of its figurines at varied points downstairs and up, moved into position between a child's forefinger and thumb with an authoritative, adult-aping voice. If you looked through the windows, all was as it should have been. As a family, at least as our family, we were doing precisely what you might have expected: my mother at a tilt over the clothes basket in the kitchen, her face flushed from being upside down and from its precarious proximity to the iron resting on the board between shirts. (She was searching for a pair of matching evening socks for her husband who eyed himself sidelong in the mirror as he shaved in the bathroom upstairs.) I was on my bed, supine, one leg crossing the other at the knee, attempting again to get beyond page three of *To the Lighthouse* by Virginia Woolf, which my father had given me for my birthday several years before, along with *The Dog It Was That Died* and a miniature dictionary – the sort you find in gimmicky shops, but my father having never frequented these, was tickled by its novelty. I had begun reading not just for my own advancement but so that I would have something to discuss with him; I wanted to talk to him but I didn't know what we could talk about. During the day I'd write things down to say to him at home, but my timing never seemed right.

I looked bookish, lying there, my face behind its covers, but my thoughts had long left the words and had travelled down to the hand tugging at my belly and were contemplating what routine I could develop to make it concave. The Frog was in front of *The Simpsons*, scissoring *The Irish Times* Crosaire Crossword he'd completed to add to his date-ordered collection. Pie was in the kitchen making flapjacks for her Christian evening. Ollie was away, travelling through Thailand, let's put him behind the house somewhere.

None of us, apart from our mother, would have known where my father was going that evening – to give some talk or lecture perhaps, but certainly we would have been unaware and uninterested in the time, precise location or theme – all of which we would subsequently be unable to forget – an eight o'clock lecture on linguistics in the Edmund Burke Theatre in Trinity and back to the Malones' for kedgeree.

I rolled myself off the bed, lolling with boredom over the edge, letting *To The Lighthouse* fall unmarked to the floor, and sat in front of the mirror, where I sang the bits I could remember of 'Nothing Compares To You', scrutinizing my face to see what I could possibly do to make it more like Sinead O'Connor's.

Trying to visualize myself bald, I shuffled upstairs to the loo. 'Do, do, do, do' the little blonde figurine in checked shirt and white knickers hopped up the ladder and through a hole in the ceiling.

When I turned the door handle of the bathroom it wouldn't give. The rest of our family would shout in this position, startled at the possibility of being exposed in whatever state of undress they were in, or whatever it was they were up to. Silence.

'Who's in there?'

'Does it matter who's in there?' My father replied, his voice cast back from the steamed-up mirror and quietly angry.

I supposed it didn't.

My newfound discipline and conformity – I was holding on to my job in the Civil Service, I was staying in and reading the books he had given me, I was contributing to housekeeping – had, instead of bringing us closer, created a greater division between my father and me, and he was becoming ever more distant. I had given up rebelling and didn't understand why this hadn't made him happy. Wasn't this what he required of me? Perhaps it was because he was so accustomed to seeing me in one way that it was asking too much of his facial muscles to request that they reconfigure in some other, more positive position. Or maybe he had seen it too many times before to believe I was really trying to change – just another one of my superficial attempts, like those carefully drawn timetables, to make a success of things when it seemed inevitable that I would fail.

My mother agreed to drive that evening so that my father could have a drink. Ready first as usual, she idly adjusted her blouse in the hall mirror, pleading wearily with her husband to hurry up and addressing half-hearted instructions to us, but in the direction of her chest, where a bit of dirt had caught her eye.

There was that familiar smell of something burning when my mother sat on the edge of my bed that night, her hands cupping its source – a mug of hot milk – on her lap. She had come home ahead of my father because he and Mr Malone had entered into some fierce debate and she had left them to it. He would take a taxi.

The Malones liked to stay up late. She told me again how one evening when they had come for dinner at our house, they had overstayed their welcome and were still there at three in the morning and she had snuck off to bed only to find my father hovering in the bedroom with the same idea. Agreeing that they couldn't both go to bed and leave the guests downstairs, they suggested to them that they return for brunch the following day, which they duly did, driving from home in their pyjamas.

It had been a wonderful evening, 'with lots of fuss made of your father', Mum said. *The Sunday Times* were keen to do an interview with him too. She kissed me goodnight on the forehead.

A foghorn had woken me some time later. I became reluctantly preoccupied with anticipating its next low moan and was unable to get back to sleep. Was it foggy that night? I cleared some condensation from my window and looked out over the low roof of the playroom at smudged street lights and house lights and the mist spreading low and ghostly over Saint Killian's field.

On my way downstairs to the kitchen for something to drink, I felt a draught coming through the hall. The front door had swung fully open to the wild night of black trees swaying about in the garden, the gravel glistening with dew on the drive. As I closed it I heard the jingle of keys; dangling from the keyhole were my father's set – identifiable as his because of the heavy study door key he took with him everywhere. I imagined what sort of state he must have been in to have not noticed either of these things and felt sorry for Mum, though he probably hadn't woken her; he would have gone to sleep in the spare room.

My movement set the house in motion. Because she had heard noise downstairs and was always competitive about being the first up and about in the mornings – Mum appeared moments later in her dressing gown, eyes puffy through lack of sleep, the skin of her cold hot milk clinging to the cup's lip and stained with the previous evening's lipstick. Above us, the Frog commenced his sit-ups: two hundred and fifty every day, the carpet worn from friction and testament to his discipline.

I told Mum about the keys and the opened front door. 'Your father was probably just a little tight, I mean a little tired,' she said. The morning continued as normal. We were instructed not to wake him. Pie sang in the shower, I set off for the office, the Frog, moving in fits and starts, rode his bike up to college.

At ten-thirty my mother climbed the stairs, treading heavily on the return with the weight of the tray holding my father's breakfast: a small pot of tea, a silver strainer for the leaves, porridge and brown sugar, an orange, and a knife. The knife wasn't for his orange – he would bite the top from this and peel the skin off in one unbroken coil – it would be employed to slice open his post. Talking to alert him as she balanced the tray on one forearm, using her free hand to turn the handle, and her foot to shove the door out of the way, my mother entered the spare room.

'Morning, pet.'

'Eric?'

Neither of the two single beds had been disturbed. She put the tray on the nearest one and called his name again outside the bathroom, knocking on the door. He wouldn't have been in there; he always used the other bathroom on the landing, preferring its layout and easterly light – better for shaving, he said.

A phone call was made to the Malones – they would have been phoned either way that day to thank them for the previous evening's entertainment and the first thing my mother did was just that. It was only when Mr Malone alluded to the speech my father had made that she asked if he had stayed with them as though it was something that she might have very stupidly mislaid. Mr Malone, consulting Mrs Malone who was now in the background, said he had left at two-thirtyish and was intending to walk home. This was entirely feasible from Baggot Street to Ballsbridge, though it was a foggy night in February. He must have come home, put his keys in the front door and realized that he had forgotten something. She phoned his office to see if he might have stayed there somewhere, in the sick room perhaps, and gone straight to work without returning. His secretary said she hadn't heard from him, but that she was expecting him in for a meeting that morning. She then tried the yacht club to no avail.

My mother, practical and positive and always wanting to make light of negative events, sat at the kitchen table and worked her way through her diary to see if she might have missed something. Both the cross door and the door to the playroom were wide open to hear the doorbell. Ollie phoned home that morning and Mum answered on the first ring, now getting a little concerned. He was so enthusiastic as he recounted tales of his travels around Koh Samui that she didn't have the heart to say anything about my father to him. There had to be a very simple explanation. He had been in high good form the previous night and had spoken of his latest achievements with some pride.

I was first home from work that afternoon (in the habit of not starting too early or staying too late). My mother was climbing the front steps when I came through the drive. She stumbled on the top step as I walked up behind her.

'Now please don't panic, pet,' she said, sounding already irritated that I had overreacted to whatever it was she was about to say, 'but your father didn't come home last night.'

*

The child playing with the doll's house gets frustrated because she can't get a figure to do what she wants it to. She flails her arms around till all the figurines are scattered, lying on their sides or tumbling out of the house altogether, with the tiny wooden bunk beds and chairs.

15

Moment

We walked in the Blue Garden of Mount Stewart, my father and I, with the air from Strangford Lough cool across wet roads and fields. Both of us were quiet, absorbed in our own thoughts.

My path led towards an ornate stone pavilion, nestled and tangled in wisteria, leaned-in to an ancient stone wall. In the half-light as I approached and my eyes strained for definition, I saw there was something inside.

Closer it became clear – two white doves, perched and preening, on the back of an old wooden bench. Still as a garden statue I watched them nibble and kiss: white in black, framed in wooden hut green, fans of feather, softness and gentle caress. One dove seemed the more attentive, the other quietly accepting, sidestepping lightly along the backrest.

I retreated silently. My father had stopped farther back and was consulting an information board, bent forward, hands clasped behind his back. Carefully, I got his attention and signalled him to me, finger on my lips, another pointing towards the shelter.

He offered me his camera. I slipped the strap over my head to secure it without him having to remind me. Inching forward again in a crouch, seriousness on my face, stealth in my approach, I squinted, eyes readjusting, into the dark, private interior.

One dove remained on the bench, quiet, lost it seemed in the moment I had missed. The other lay still, face down on the cold, cracked tiled floor. Dead.

I woke from this dream, or was it a memory, to a radio announcement that Nelson Mandela was free. My father was missing and Nelson Mandela was free. I must have fallen asleep with it on. It had been two days. The police had been contacted, the news spread, relatives called around. Adjectives were tossed about – surreal, baffling, most peculiar – along with theories as to what might have happened. My father had been dependable and a man of habit all his life – perhaps he had been taken against his will like that dentist who'd had his fingers chopped off, or was lying injured somewhere. Had there been anything he was worried about? The police wanted to know. Had he been behaving unusually? Might he have gone to Sea Spray without telling anyone?

It seemed inappropriate to be having my eyes tested that day, but an appointment to see whether I would be a suitable candidate for Eye Laser surgery had been made months earlier and my mother encouraged me to attend it. It was what I'd asked for, for my twenty-first birthday. My father was nervous of anything to do with eyes and left it up to her to make a decision about it, as he had begun to do with anything concerning me. We were supposed to do normal things in the belief that normality itself would be restored and life would continue as before.

On the bus back from an initial consultation I forgot about the crisis at home and momentarily indulged in the news that I was a suitable candidate for Eye Laser surgery – by the age of twenty-one I would finally be able to see clearly. Observing the world around me, I tried to imagine what it would look like in real life, edges defining themselves, light illuminating.

On a street corner a man was tying a woman's shoelace. She held her foot out like a child; he was bent below her, on one knee. I couldn't see his face, but from the back he looked to be in his late fifties: his head was bald at the crown with only a smattering of grey hair remaining around the sides. Every old man I see reminds me of my father – I thought of that Patrick Kavanagh poem I'd learnt at school. She looked younger, more attractive than him.

I squinted at them, now below me, as the bus pulled into a stop. They didn't appear to be talking; I still couldn't see the man's face but he had lifted his head and was smiling up at her. There was an intimacy in their body language and a closeness suggested by the silence between them. He stood up, kissed her on the neck, took her hand and turned around. I watched them as the bus pulled away. I looked again. Harder.

It was my father. I was up, out of my seat, shaking and looking back. It was my father for sure. On a street corner, on the wrong side of town, in a raincoat I hadn't seen before. I strained to keep my eyes on them as their faces faded. My stomach was churning, the motion of the bus making me queasy, other passengers, noticing that I was startled, stared openly.

The secret drawer in his desk, the locked study door. And he was missing so often, so often abroad, on business somewhere, arriving home from somewhere else, unavailable, backing out of the kitchen and away from us with his dinner on a tray. He was the man who wasn't there, and now I knew why. I contemplated getting off the bus and marching back down the road to confront them.

Maybe I'd been wrong, they had looked so comfortable with each other, such a pair. Surely my father would have been more discreet, cleverer? It was impossible to think of him with someone other than Mum. To imagine him skulking around backstreets with some stranger was ludicrous – I must have been wrong.

While my mother searched the clothes basket for his socks, he was out getting cosy with some cow. He wasn't hers. He belonged to us. He hadn't been in trouble or injured at all; he had abandoned us intentionally. Did we drive him to it? Or maybe Mum did by putting on a few pounds as she aged, pounds she should have burned trudging up the stairs with his porridge and post each morning for the last twenty-five years. Or maybe she knew, had known all along.

This chance sighting had given me moral ground for the first time in my life. If this was true, I was innocent; he was guilty. I'd caught him out. He always had the final say on my behaviour and now I had full voice on his. I was the adult, him the treacherous adolescent. I had ammunition. I was going to confront him.

As I put my key in the front door, it opened. Mrs Hampton appeared behind it in my mother's apron. It looked newer on her somehow, less used. She'd tied the strings twice around her pink cashmere sweater. She had rubber gloves on, her sweater rolled up to her elbows and a J-cloth in her hand. She'd been clearing up after us; trying to make herself useful.

This was the scene I had pictured and dreaded forever: a stranger in our house because there had been a crisis. When someone other than one of your family answers the door, there is immediate cause for concern.

The lights had not been switched on to welcome guests; they'd been slapped on in panic as people ran upstairs and down, because there had been an emergency; because something was not right.

They had found my father, Mrs Hampton said. My mother was in the hospital with him.

16

The tock of time measured

There was an armchair we used to drive past on family holidays on our way to Connemara; an overstuffed, rose-coloured, lopsided old armchair, discarded in the Strawberry Beds, far from anywhere. For us, squeezed and bickering in the back seat, wedged between my father's typewriter, boxes of groceries and the wine cooler, and flanked by cellophane-wrapped suit jackets hung curtain-like over the windows, it was a landmark that told us we were still a miserably long way from being nearly there.

To my father this armchair represented utopia; its remote location the utter bliss of solitude. On long car journeys, more than at any other time, he found our presence infuriating: a ceaseless digging of knees into the back of his seat, the whines about toys we'd forgotten to pack, needing the toilet, about the poor baby lambs on that hill near Roundstone that murderers like my father were happy to eat. It became 'Dad's armchair' and was acknowledged as such by us, by my mother, by all his friends and even by my father who grinned at his own eccentricity.

I imagined him in his armchair: legs crossed at the knee the way thin men sit, slippered feet underneath, trembling with restlessness. Brows arched furiously over some dusty tome on his lap, anticipating disruption, lowering slowly when no disruption comes. His foot will cease its motion as he becomes engrossed, mouth relaxing into a pout. The periodic rub of his handkerchief like a duster about his face, the need to stand every so often to re-configure his nether regions, the clearing of his throat as he sits again, eyes scanning lines of type to find his place.

That's where he was found, in the armchair, unconscious and suffering from hypothermia. The barman from the Strawberry Hall who came across him thought at first that he was having a nap, but he seemed the wrong shape to be asleep. If my father needed to sleep he would have made himself a hot-water bottle and a hot whiskey, carried both upstairs with his wireless wedged under his arm, washed his face and behind his ears, undressed, got into his pyjamas, removed his wristwatch, taken his slippers off and positioned them under his bed in readiness for the following morning, got into bed, propped his pillow behind his back and settled into some P.G. Wodehouse.

They had put my father in a hospital gown – a flimsy white robe imprinted with cheery, multicoloured writing – and had tied it loosely around his shoulders, exposing too much of him. His chest, which we were accustomed to seeing darkly tanned and freckled by the sun, was pasty and swollen, like uncooked sausages. It seemed almost womanly in its expanse and too intimate to be on view. His glasses had been removed; the skin around his closed lids was sunken, accentuating the pop-eyed bulges beneath. His hair was flyaway on the pillow and needed to be combed; it gave him a befuddled look. Froth had gathered around his mouth that was gagged by a tube like a snorkel. He looked toppled, a collapsed snowman.

It felt voyeuristic to be viewing him; it was like walking into his bedroom without knocking to find him in a state of undress. There was an uneasiness too – I knew that I had mistaken the man on the street for him, but the bad aftertaste was still there, it was as though we'd shared a secret, the way you feel awkward when you've dreamt about someone and happen to bump into them the following day.

Things had been done to him that he'd had no say in and couldn't voice an objection to: the prodding, the poking, the high-pitched pips of the machines, the proximity of the patient next door, the unctions and ointments in the sanitized air, us standing at the bottom of his bed, like useless sentinels, obstacles in the way of doctors.

My mother felt his fingers move. Her hand in his looked old: stiff and peppered with liver spots and risen veins. The nail on her wedding finger was chipped; the ring pushing against the knuckle was greasy and coated with candle wax. My father's hands were smooth and capable in contrast, his fingers, wooden puppet sticks, the nails neat, square and clean; perfect half-moon-shaped cuticles. They were hands that appeared always to be washed and ready for the meticulous examination of old coins, rare books, of fragile things.

No, the intensive care nurse wouldn't call it a coma; they were waiting, hoping, for him to wake up. He had had a stroke further complicated by severe exposure. He couldn't breathe by himself but his heart was still beating. His badly damaged feet – blistered, bruised toes, hardened skin at the heels – suggested that he had probably walked a great distance. She explained the electrodes affixed to his chest, the urinary catheter, the oxygen censor on his finger. She smelt of potato crisps. She encouraged me to speak to him; told me that hearing was the last sense to go.

I was suddenly aware of the room being too bright – it brought to mind the junior school classroom where I'd had to stand in front of everyone and spell the word 'because'. I was numb; I was being watched, no words would come. The nurse had been quick to answer all of my questions except for the last: I asked her if she thought my father was going to recover. I would have to speak to the doctors, she said.

Life was suspended. The family assembled round the kitchen table as though it was Christmas or one of our birthdays. The phone rang incessantly, as did the door-bell: neighbours with quiches and questions and concern. Mum went into overdrive with things to be done. My sister helped her, but when people enquired after my father's condition she would crumple. My little brother set about doing the jobs my father would ordinarily have done – raking leaves, fixing loose door handles, sorting files out, being frustrated with mess. When we were at home we felt we should be at the hospital; when there we wanted to be at home.

My twenty-first birthday coincided with the fifth night my father spent in intensive care. A cake was purchased, a pot of tea was made, place settings of mallard ducks in reeds were arranged around the kitchen table and wiped over with an elderly J-cloth, coating everything with tracks of bubbled grease. The lights were switched off, 'Happy Birthday' was sung, on that occasion, without Pie's harmony, the usual spray of saliva over cake, candles were plucked from the sponge and saved to be recycled for the next cause for celebration. The phone rang ceaselessly.

We gathered again in the waiting room and talked of CAT scans and tea, of brain damage and tea, of critical illness and do you want some milk? Pie had recited the Hail Mary ten times on the hour, for nine hours, over five days, and still he hadn't woken up.

My mother searched for the positive in the progressively gloomier prognoses of consultants. 'Where there's life there's hope,' was her mantra that week. I saw him coming home, jolted through gravel in a wheelchair, high shoes, plaid rug, head slumped on shoulder, from which position he would have to be spoon-fed.

Months earlier I had asked him to type up a short story I'd attempted for a Dublin magazine – a first draft of a piece I'd written about the man in London who lived upstairs. He agreed to it readily, perhaps because I appeared to be focusing for once on something other than Max Factor and men.

He had burst into the kitchen, looking red-faced and shocked, the way he had done the day he told us that his great friend Mr McNellis was dead. 'Excellent!' he declared, handing my story back. I held it, hands shaking, as he pointed out some minor grammatical errors. When he had gone, I read over it again, embarrassed but brimming with pride. On the last page he had made a mistake: instead of the word 'field' he had typed 'fiels'. It was impossible to imagine his mind being gone. Physical fragility I could adjust more easily to – he had never been physically strong.

I remembered a childhood riding lesson: I was on a Shetland pony, far too far from the ground, whimpering when it stretched its neck to chew at some grass, wanting to get down. Why was my father holding on to the pony? It was his freckled head in front of me, his thin hands wrestling with the reins. Why was he even there that day? It wasn't his sort of outing, and I certainly didn't trust him; he hated animals and I knew they sensed that sort of thing. He seemed as perplexed as I was and cursed the imposition, the muck on his brogues, the reek of the beasts pacing behind him.

My ambition that week was to become an international show jumper. I loved everything to do with ponies: the sun-warm saddles, the silver stirrups, the straps to become proficient in the adjusting of, bridles hung on whitewashed walls, the pungency of manure, the round, hollow sound of shod hooves on cobble-stones. Riding, on the other hand, terrified me. I was petrified of being so far from the ground, startled at how I lurched from side to side when I nudged my pony to move.

The Shetland became agitated, snorting, bobbing his head at the irritation of flies. I groped about in the coarse hair of his mane, trying to keep control. My hat was too big and itchy and I was unhappy about the button it was missing at its crown, and my legs were stretched uncomfortably over the heat of the pony's stomach as if I were on a Space Hopper, except that I was now the toy and the live, sweating animal under-neath was in control. The palomino that Pie was riding nuzzled up to my pony and the tethered sheepdog in the courtyard began to complain. I whined at my father to do something.

I imagine he made some attempts to pacify it, but whipped his hand away when it took a step forward or wrestled to be free. With a final lurch my mount took off. Its neck was up, ears erect. I pictured its wild eyes beneath me, its huge, grass-stained teeth bared. I bumped about screaming on its back, lunging in the squeaking leather of the saddle, with my father in a half-run alongside us, shouting bizarre instructions as he squelched through cowpats. I had never seen him advance at anything other than a brisk walk – this was even more frightening to me.

He couldn't keep up, he was helpless, he let go, the reins slipped and my beast was free. We hurtled towards a hazy array of high hedges, farm gates and dark trees, my father's voice fading. I slid off the saddle; my riding hat fell first. I could hear him cursing behind me in the slow motion of the fall, then the dizzy rush towards me of boots and voices, the thwack of a bloody nose, a thicket of brambles, a hard heavy thud on cracked soil.

17

Darkness visible

My mother, to the left in the foreground, had her hands joined on her lap and was sitting upright, with her eyes turned, as always, towards my father. Behind her, Ollie squinted, badly hung-over. The Frog stared out beside him with an intense, sinister glare. In the middle Pie smiled sweetly. Her eyes were not only strong, but they were a different colour from the rest of ours. I would tell her she was almost certainly adopted. And there was me, in profile, looking down and away from the camera, doing whatever was necessary to disguise my lazy eye. In front of all of us, beside my mother, my father peered out at the world through thick-rimmed tortoiseshell glasses.

After surgery I would feel disconcerted, the nurse said, as though I were walking underwater. I tried to visualize that. She handed me a Valium and a styrofoam cup and squeaked off in her sensible shoes. I hate when medical people warn you about these things to make you feel better: telling you it might hurt a little when they knew it would hurt a lot. There wasn't enough water to wash the pill down; it was lodged somewhere in my windpipe. I swallowed hard with my neck tilted back, wondering how soon I might feel its effect and how effective it would be.

My teeth left their imprint on the lip of the cup. Squat, square, like fat little milk teeth, was how Patsy described them once. They had got that way from grinding. It was a very common occurrence in highly strung, high-achieving perfectionists, my dentist had said. He admired my father and had assumed, like everyone else, that I possessed the same academic genius.

Disconcerted. I was jittery with trepidation already. For one thing the hospital didn't look as I'd hoped; the corridors should have been bleached and empty of any suggestion of illness or impending mortality – wheelchairs, holy water, unmade blankets on trolleys, moss-coloured waiting-room chairs, meals on wheels, wilting flowers in porcelain sinks – empty of everything in fact but urgent, competent doctors in lab coats on their way to fix people with their technologically advanced and shining steel machines.

The walls of the room were that particular shade of hearing-aid pink you find in draughty toilets with rusting cisterns at the back of countryside pubs. The red-tiled floor was carrying me on trains of thought I didn't want to take: down our road and back to the MacDermots' house. There were tiles like those in their kitchen, below the Aga where scorched tea towels were draped and beneath the dumb waiter in the corner that smelt of overcooked cabbage and underarms in house-coats. Old Mrs MacDermot appeared in pointy-edged glasses and pinned hair behind the wheel of a Rolls-

Royce. She belonged to the past even when alive. Her husband beside her, dead too, with his beef-red face, belted mackintosh, wispy, angel-white hair.

I sucked on my cheeks. A listing portrait of Pope John Paul II, a switched-off television; my reflection lost in its blank face, a black shape in outline, like the negative of a photograph, in the shadow of a window. It took me along another track, back to the boredom of dead Sundays at home: TV unplugged, a *Waltons* special cut short following a fight about homework, my forehead pressed in defiance against the window streaked with grey rain, taking solace in its cool condensation. Then prone on the floor, peering idly under the sofa at a half-nibbled Fig Roll and a tiny, shining silver thing: the missing boot from the Monopoly set. Once searched for everywhere – under cushions, below the carefully lifted board – now redundant, its discovery irrelevant.

I closed my eyes. I was gone but the reflection of the

window slid across my lids. Haloes, double vision, floaters, false tears, starbursts, blinkers, blurred vision, blindness. I imagined myself as a swollen-ankled old woman hobbling through the high street with an important letter to send, mistaking the modern bin outside the newsagent's for a post box, slipping the envelope in my arthritic hands through the opening, and hobbling home almost happy.

I used to meet a blind man nearly every day on my way to work. Instead of crossing the road at the pedestrian lights, where the audible bleeps would have given him safe egress, he would march on a few yards and stride out into the rush of traffic, shuffling through horns and the slam of brakes, sightless in a world of sound. I helped him whenever I saw him, the two of us venturing out together – the going blind leading the gone. Uncle Arthur had an eye operation to fix one of his – something went wrong and now the two looked out from opposing sides of his head. At Christmas dinner he'd stand poised with a carving knife. 'How many for turkey?' he'd say, one eye riveted on the cornice above the wall, the other roaming the garden.

A man sitting opposite me in the waiting room was perpetually clearing his throat, as if he were about to make an important announcement. I was probably irritating him as much with my incessant blinking – I wanted to use all my blinks up before I got in so I would feel less tempted to when it was critical that I hold my eyes still. Beside him, a comfortable sort of woman read a book – the sort of woman you see at a supermarket with a child on her hip, comparing the merits of various brands of toilet paper.

The pair of tennis-shod feet poking out between curtains worried me. The surgery had been performed on the person behind it and they were in the recovery stage. But why weren't they moving? Why did they need to lie down? Why was it necessary to keep them concealed?

I said a quick prayer to my namesake, Saint Lucy, patron saint of the blind and those with eye trouble. Lucy means light, and has the same root as 'lucid', which means 'clear, radiant, understandable' – three agreeable words. According to legend, the emperor Diocletian plucked out poor Lucy's eyes and gave them back to her on a dish, but God took pity on her and restored her sight so it all worked out happily in the end. I was impressed with myself for remembering this fact. And there was another: after the completion of Saint Basil's Cathedral in Moscow, Ivan the Terrible plucked out the eyes of his architects, ensuring that no other building so exquisite could be raised again.

My old swimming teacher had only one eye; the other was made of glass. I used to worry as she fished around with that pole, that it would fall out and into the water and become a bubble that one of us might swallow by mistake, or worse, have to retrieve. The pole made me think of that fishing rod flung back on the pier that tore out a child's eye. The pier reminded me of the sea and that seal who used to balance fish on its nose for a heron, till the bird swooped down one day, confused the seal's shining eye for his fish supper, stole it and flew away.

I winced and squeezed my lids shut.

I wondered whether everyone else in the room was counting on the same radical transformation as I was. *Eye Laser surgery changed my life.* I'd read another article since about a woman who, prior to surgery, had had a recurring dream about a filthy toilet, blocked, with brown sewage overflowing from its lip. Once she'd had the operation, she left her job, ended a dysfunctional relationship and never dreamt of the putrid toilet again. Her boyfriend had been older than her and had hoped she'd stay myopic as he was scared that she'd leave him when she saw what he looked like in real life.

I would leave the Civil Service and become a famous journalist, poet or perhaps a writer, having lively and witty dinner debates with my father, when he got better, about all aspects of literature and current affairs. My strawberry flans would be drooled over at coffee mornings, my serves would finally go in. I would give strangers directions clearly and confidently without having to feel for the watch on my left hand. Magical things would begin to unfold just as soon as I had clear vision.

I would visit the air-raid shelter near Palmerstown Park and see it for the first time. Palmerstown Park and Pie and a sense of my father, not a sighting of him, or the sound of his voice, but a sense of him standing on the soft grass behind us: his walking shoes and trouser legs. Watching us on the seesaw, self-consciously playing, aware of his eyes on us and trying to do what small children should do. There was talk of visiting the giant doll's house in one of the Georgian homes on the square whose lit windows I glimpsed from the swing when it swung high over the railings, through the clear, frosty evening. But no, it was dark; no, we'd visit the doll's house another day.

No more glasses. The day before, Dolores from the office said they really suited me. Looking at them made me feel vulnerable: they were badly scratched and I'd had to sellotape the crack at the bridge.

Though the doctor said that they would look identical to my current pair, I couldn't help daydreaming about new eyes. I hoped they would be fiercely, exquisitely blue, like Tatum O'Neal's in that shot where she's swimming underwater in Tahiti. Not only would I be able to see through them, they would be matching and dewy and deeply set and my new eyelashes would be thick and black and wet looking. Not really my eyes at all, when I thought about it, but still recognizably me.

I liked that my doctor was brusque and matter of fact; I found this lack of bedside manner oddly reassuring – as if he knew precisely what he was doing and was too busy thinking complicated thoughts to waste his time with small talk. He had a thick black moustache that curled up at the ends. When I first saw *Magnum* on TV I developed a brief but intense fondness for men with moustaches; now I found them comical, like the false ones that came attached to plastic glasses and a big nose, the sort Uncle Pat used to wear to my birthday parties.

The door of the surgery opened and a goggle-eyed woman appeared, guided under the forearm by the squeaky-shoed nurse. She had that defenceless, naked look of the newly bereaved. The still short-sighted watched her, freshly perturbed. She looked like a giant alien bug, her features pulled and bunched by the tape that held the plastic shields in place.

As my doctor swivelled forward on his stool, positioning himself behind my head, the nurse removed my glasses and used a foot pedal to lower me on a reclining chair. I was aware of a third person in the room, in the corner, behind a computer screen. Their swift, seamless movements made me nervous. The nurse was trying to distract me with something – holidays? Work? I can't remember, but I wanted her to stop: she was making me more anxious.

Everything was moving too fast. I needed another conversation about the procedure – a final outlining of the risks. In another moment a numbing drop was placed in each of my eyes and something cold prised my lids open: I couldn't blink if I'd wanted to. *A Clockwork Orange.*

'You will lose your vision for a moment,' the doctor said, manoeuvring a heavy machine with a microscope attached. I felt a pressure around my eye socket, and then I was blind: a tunnelling blackness that went on too long. In my blindness I saw my father, down the road, lying in blackness too, unable to move, bound up by the tubes and monitors and machines that were keeping him alive.

Positioning the laser over my eye, the doctor told me to stare at the light. Was this when the flap in my cornea would be lifted? I was petrified of developing an itch. The laser ticked as it worked. There was a smell of singed hair. 'Twenty-five.' The man in the corner began counting backwards. 'Twenty-four. Twenty-three.' The laser pulsed around my eye. 'Twenty-two. Twenty-one. Twenty.' Roads Less Travelled job gone. 'Nineteen. Eighteen.' Freewheeling home from the Hellfire Club. 'Seventeen. Sixteen.' Indelible dye on the bathroom door. 'Fifteen. Fourteen. Thirteen. Twelve.' My father counting down as he climbed the stairs.

18

Dragonflies draw flame

Armed, for the first time, with a legitimate excuse for being in bed at three o'clock in the afternoon, I drew the curtains, curled up under the bedclothes in my goggles and waited for my eyes to heal. They teared and streamed and smarted as though an arc light shone on them. I couldn't get comfortable; I wriggled and squirmed, put my head under the pillow. They felt filled with jagged bits of grit – I was desperate to rub them.

I could wait no longer; I had to try out my new eyes. Pulling the covers from my head I squinted out through the perforations of my plastic shields. I couldn't make out anything clearly; all was smeared and cloudy as if I were looking through the base of a jam jar.

I pulled the blanket back over my head. It had been a disappointing first view of the world. It was essential that my new sight be noticeably different. Not just for my sake but for everyone else's. I felt under pressure for it to be a miraculous thing: a means of explaining why nothing had gone according to plan so far but how, from this day, everything would be different. I wanted to be elated. Anything less than that would be, aside from disappointing, embarrassing in an odd way. It would be like coming back from a trip to Mauritius without a suntan and reporting that your holiday had just been all right.

Aunt Maureen, my father's sister whom we rarely saw, had volunteered to look after me during my recovery while the rest of the family went back and forth to the hospital. In contrast to her clipped appearance – pointed shoes, a buttoned-up coat, a needle-sharp black umbrella – Aunt Maureen was loquacious and fluid of speech. She worked as a librarian; all the words she had to suppress during her day tumbled out when she was in company. She had little confidence that what she had to say would be of any consequence to anyone else, yet she felt entitled to fill in silences and would talk in a voice that sounded further and further away as she drifted off on her stories, frequently carrying on a rambling monologue when everyone else had left the room.

Perched at the far end of my bed with her cup and saucer of tea – always slightly wary of me – she talked about her holidays. Specifically, what she had eaten on each day and evening of a recent trip to Salzburg, in tedious, mind-numbing detail.

'For lunch on Sunday we had the grilled salmon fillets with parsley potatoes and cooked spinach, followed by an apple strudel, or did we have sachertorte? No, the sachertorte was Monday. Or was it? Yes that's it. On Monday evening I had some Kaiserschmarren, a sort of omelette with raisins and plum compote. We tried out some Wiener Melange with our breakfast on Tuesday.'

She used her index finger to punch some crumbs from a ginger snap on her saucer and fed them onto her tongue, while no doubt trying to recall what they had eaten for breakfast on Wednesday.

I knew she had been on holiday for ten days; there were seven days of meals still to go. The sound of the phone ringing should have been a relief – instead it made me want to be sick, pins and needles prickling my scalp.

Aunt Maureen answered it – I went down the stairs after her, feeling my way through the haze. She held the receiver away from her mouth and shook it as if she wanted to rid herself of the person on the other end of the line. 'I see,' she said, 'I understand.' At the end of an equine nose were nostrils permanently chapped from the abrasion of a handkerchief. 'Bye bye bye bye bye bye,' she said as she hung up.

It was the hospital. She would go. I should stay at home, she said, fussing about her handbag for car keys. She looked up when I told her I wanted to go with her and eyed me steadily.

My stomach tightened. I knew what she meant. It was what I had been privately obsessing about since my father got sick – that it was mostly my fault he had gone missing in the first place. I had run him ragged over the years and now I'd finally worn him out. He had said himself often enough that I'd put ten years on his life.

I had to see him to say sorry. I wanted to tell him I loved him, to say goodbye. He was my father. I wanted to see him one last time. I peeled off my goggles.

We careered over speed bumps along our road. I had

the brief sense of being important when she broke a red light at the church. The car was too warm and stuffy; there was a talcum-powdery smell. I should have sat in the front; I wanted the window rolled down, I couldn't breathe. Outside, a man at a bus stop lifted one shoe, then the other, inspecting them for dog dirt. All Aunt Maureen had said was that my poor old father was weak.

He had been dead for twenty minutes when I saw him. No one said the word dead, but he was shrunken and tiny amongst sheets, curled up stiff in foetal position with his arms bent and his hands under his head like a child. His face was turned away, half buried into a pillow as if to say he'd had too much pain. His lips were scabbed; he looked thirsty and stunned. There was a small sticking plaster on the inside of his elbow; the skin around it was the colour of a bruised potato. On his tiny wrist was a plastic bracelet, the kind you see on a newborn baby. His legs protruded from the hospital gown like a lady's and were waxy and jaundiced and bone-snap thin.

I lay down on the bed and hugged the rigid shell. I wasn't aware of anyone else in the room but we all must have been there. I was too big for him – my shape, my bulk, around a shrivelled thing. I whispered to him that I loved him though I knew it was too late. He was gone. He would never see my new eyes, my new start. He would never be proud of me.

*

We walked in a clump, the whole family, along a narrow corridor past the waiting room where relations, reflected in night-darkened windows, stood speechless, past a statue of Jesus outside the chapel, pitying us from His plastic cross – to hell with Him and the rest of them. My little brother put his hand on my shoulder and held it there. A heavy pressure, disproportionate, it seemed, to his size.

We squeezed into Aunt Maureen's car, on top of knees, sitting forward, crushed against doors: a crammed-in cargo of misery.

On my mother's lap was a large green bin bag containing my father's possessions, momentarily illuminated by the lights of the car behind ours. Bundled, not folded, and for everyone to see: his underpants; his fountain pen; his favourite Aran sweater, cut jaggedly down the centre; the book of poetry by Hopkins, which had been wedged into his jacket pocket when they found him in the armchair; an unwound watch.

19

Eyes not his

After ten days of trips to the hospital, trips back and forth to answer the door, up and down to pick up the phone, to early morning Masses and back with briquettes lugged up the front steps, fires set for visitors, a drain unblocked, a mouse trapped, my father's socks located, paired, put away, soups made, floors washed, flowers arranged, silver polished, hot milk boiled before bed, my mother finally fell down.

She fell over the mop and bucket on the back stairs, making a sound I hadn't heard before – a discordant shriek – the sort of screech the tumble dryer made before it blew a fuse. She didn't get up straight away, as she would have done ordinarily, brushing dust from her knees, scolding herself by her Christian name for being clumsy. She stayed where she was. I found her on hands and knees like a dog, looking up at me with a face stretched and flushed through strands of silver hair. 'That hurt,' she said. I couldn't remember her ever complaining about physical pain before. Then she wept, tears dripping onto her hands. The light bulb on the back stairs had gone, there was a greasy patch on the carpet where something had spilt. My mother was on the floor. There was no possible way through all of this. It was hopeless.

The doorbell rang and life continued.

Maura from the office was on the doorstep in charcoal tones, holding a box in her arms from which she unpacked an assortment of crocheted black shawls reminiscent of rural Ireland during the famine. She had brought them for us in case we didn't have anything suitable to wear at the funeral, she explained, in the whispery croak she reserved for occasions such as these.

The cat – a new cat, some stray – darted unimpeded up the stairs. He had only been dead three days and already my father's rules were being flouted. Deep baths were run, shoes were worn indoors, there was a liberal usage of words he detested, words such as 'hopefully' and 'no way'. After all those years of effort, had he failed in instilling his principles in us? Had we only obeyed him out of fear rather than because we had any real understanding of why he wanted us to behave in particular ways? His standards and what he required from us seemed irrelevant on the day of his funeral, but more than that was the feeling that we were simply taking advantage of him being out somewhere – at a meeting. I still thought of him as missing.

I had a dream about my father; or rather a person I recognized as my father but who was an entirely different man. He hadn't died at all, but had moved out and left us, and had been missing for several years. He came back younger, unshaven, without glasses, his peppermint-blue shirt rolled up to the elbows and worn loose, out over his trousers. Down on his luck and living in some basement, he pestered me to accept him. He was the opposite of himself. I'd dreamt about the alter ego of my mother once too. A scowling, hollow-cheeked woman, sucking on a cigarette, in stone-washed denim, one foot bent behind her against a factory wall.

Before my father died I had a sort of fear of death and disability and of people who had lost a family member; the sight of an empty wheelchair in the corner of a room, of Down's syndrome children in a swimming pool. I didn't want to get close to them, didn't want to be in their houses, didn't want their oppressive grief infecting me. Death wasn't so much sad as a terrifying, musty, curtains-drawn-in-the-day secret; the high-pitched requiems of choirs in ghostly lavender gardens; red-haired boys in paisley pyjamas who died in house fires; the widow in Cash Stores still in mourning, her veiled head bowed, under her arm a sliced pan; the imprint of a dead child's plimsoll on the road near the beach. And here we were, having it done to us. Not our family, I thought. Granny had been worn out and ready and we had been too young to feel the full blow of losing her. But not our giant of a father, collapsed in his prime and gone. We weren't frail or unlucky like that.

Throughout that week my eyes began to heal. For the first few days they felt strained, tight at the corners when I swivelled them to view objects sidelong, the way they feel in those waking moments of a hangover. Initially objects appeared out of focus as if squinted at through a telescope, but my eyes adjusted the longer I looked and my vision became sharper and clearer. I administered drops and examined myself in the mirror, noting any change in their appearance, distracting myself with things I hadn't considered about my face before – the downy hair on my cheeks, the lines under my eyes – until the heavy stone lurch in my stomach when thoughts of my father returned.

The cadaver in the coffin didn't look like him. He was puffed up and whiter than the body in the bed. His face framed in gathered silk, the stunned look was now serene, unreadable, and his lips had been painted and manipulated into a pleasant half-way grin that looked as though they might at any moment break into a smile. I had to look away. I was seeing too clearly, too much.

My father had one of those smiles that, because it wasn't used too often or too casually, looked beautiful when it appeared. When I made him laugh it was almost always unexpected – never when I'd memorized a joke or play-acted to put off going to bed, but occasionally when I was sulking and unaware of having said anything amusing. He'd slap his hand on the table – startling at first, yet to be defined as anger or mirth – then he would throw his mouth open, fling his head back and roar like a howler monkey, again and again, louder each time, like convulsions he seemed unable to control. I'd press my fingers over the corners of my lips to suppress my smile, to maintain my sulky repose, but secretly proud that I had made my father laugh.

I had never seen the herringbone jacket he was in – it looked incongruous, too short in the arms. The buttons gaped around his middle, its sleeves were threadbare at the cuffs. The tie he was wearing bore the emerald emblem of a rugby club – my father didn't own a sports tie, his were paisley and subdued and selected with the utmost care. The undertakers had made a mistake. They had put my father in another dead man's clothes.

A panic ensued with the funeral home being contacted, the correct clothes located and swiftly replaced. My mother told the undertakers that she would re-dress my father. My sister agreed to help. I wouldn't have been able for the job. There was a half an hour delay.

Mr Malone had laughed nervously, the way some people do, when he heard the news that my father was dead. He was the first person I recognized standing outside the church, his head straining from his shirt-collar like sausage meat – a blood knot fit to burst. Genevieve was beside him. Lachrymose at the best of times, she already had mascara smearing her cheeks. As she wiped them, the sticking plaster came lose on her hand, revealing what she'd tried for so long to conceal – old age in the shape of a liver spot.

We made our way down the aisle and under the choir, ghostly in the gallery, unseen fingers tumbling over organ keys. We passed pews of crying babies, patted backs, damp overcoats, noses blown, sputters and coughs, and took our front-of-house seats.

I was in a haze, unable to think of him, unable to

summon up any emotion but resentment towards the priest, the organ, the mourners, all of whom seemed to be forcing me to accept something I wasn't ready to.

It embarrassed me that everyone was party to the disintegration of our family unit. And we were a unit, squeezed together on our bench, pale and stunned, shoulders and knees touching. From the day my father collapsed we had begun to hug one another, a gesture that had previously felt ludicrous and insincere. In the space of ten days we had all grown up – one rough shove into adulthood.

At the end of our row was my mother. Stoic, sitting upright, almost stately with composure as strangers consoled her. She was stronger than I'd ever seen her; she was holding all of us together. I'd been so focused on trying to get my father's attention for twenty-one years, I had never considered that my mother had always been there: at school plays, tennis matches I was losing, the edge of my bed at night.

The priest, trendy and new to the parish with cowlicked hair in a pageboy style, added new emphasis to the sections of the sermon we reeled off, so that we might stop reeling them off and consider the profundity of the words we were uttering. 'Let *us* pray,' he said, stressing the 'us', and adding exaggerated pauses at particular points of the service to encourage us to ponder our faith.

'Let *us* pray,' he said, 'for the souls of all the faithful departed, in particular at *this* time *we* remember Maude Patterson' – a barnacled old aunt of ours who had been suffering from a life-threatening case of pneumonia but had made a miraculous recovery and was now sitting robust and nonplussed in the second row.

My sister, in a shoulder-padded suit – the growing bump in her belly concealed, her sheepish boyfriend in a neat suit behind us, head down – read a tongue-twister by Hopkins, voice quivering. Her hairstyle looked lopsided; too big on one side and flat on the other as though she'd slept on it. She had been to get it done that morning and for some inexplicable reason the hair-dresser had asked if she'd mind blow-drying it herself.

> As Kingfishers catch fire, dragonflies draw flame;
> As tumbled over rim in roundy wells
> Stones ring; like each tucked string tells, each hung bell's
> Bow swung finds tongue to fling out broad its name;
> Each mortal thing does one thing and the same;
> Deals out that being indoors each one dwells;
> Selves – goes itself; myself it speaks and spells
> Crying What I do is me: for that I came.

There was a communal release of breath when she finally made it, relatively successfully, to the end of the first verse. People coughed and shifted in their seats. Thank God for that.

I say more ...

The second verse began and heads were once more bowed, eyes focused on the bench in front or examining fingers, picking threads from loose hems.

I couldn't watch. I knew it was torture for her up there. She didn't want to do a reading any more than she had wanted to change the clothes of her dead father, but she had been born with something I needed: a sense of responsibility.

Lovely in limbs, and lovely in eyes not his
To the Father through the features of men's faces.

The shaking of incense over the coffin caused the smoke alarm to go off – there was a mumble of whispers, red-eyed amusement at what my father would have thought. The truth was that my father would have left the church by then – he always made sure to be gone before the enforced intimacy of shaking hands with strangers at the sign of peace. He would have been halfway home at that stage, with the Sunday newspapers under his arm.

I saw our empty house. Magpies pit-patting across the playroom roof, a swollen drip trembling from the leaking tap in the upstairs bathroom. The feeble bleep of the alarm clock coming from my room, which I'd set and then woken long before, shivering with cold, my blankets on the floor. Mum couldn't sleep either. I'd heard her pacing back and forth to the toilet, the radio on in the dark and turned low, finally giving up on sleep and opening the curtains in her room.

My father was wheeled away in his coffin. We shuffled up the aisle behind him to a great oratorio of angelic voices, rising, lifting – powerfully, gloriously, unearthly – as though his coffin might at any moment leave its trolley and float upwards, supported under its base by the fingers of cherubic angels, towards the roof that would burst suddenly open to the blinding, heavenly sunlight of eternity.

Outside the church, Alison Hampton wandered over to me, her parents supporting her under each arm. It was the first time I'd seen her since her breakdown. Her once petite frame had become solid through force-fed hospital food. On her chin was a sore that looked picked at. She didn't ask how I was, despite the occasion. Instead she talked about herself and her illness, the lilt from her voice gone. It occurred to me that up until she became ill she had been unknowable. Patsy came up while we chatted. We hugged each other stiffly, self-consciously, both of us thinking as we did, that it was the first and very last time.

Old Mrs McDermot's daughter, big and bouncy Stephanie, had gone the other way – hollow-cheeked and frail, she was suffering from bulimia. Ollie, back from his travels around the Far East with different body language and an insistence that we address him as Oliver, was in the car park talking to Billie, my old art teacher, who was there with her girlfriend. She and my brother had become friendly, often running into each other around certain venues in the city.

Back at the house there was a fuss of furniture being moved and salt fetched: Doctor Long had spilt a glass of red wine over one of the sofas, and was standing red-eared and at a loss by the piano, while women mopped up furiously around him, telling him not to worry, and men looked on offering solutions.

My parents' friends sat around a small table, reduced as they were in number and in physical size. There were fewer of them now and the ones that were left were less sure of their words and their teeth and their feet. The laughter was not so uproarious, their faces sadder in repose. That day I saw my parents' friends as ordinary people for the first time; the sort of people you pass in the shops, fumbling about for change, having hips replaced.

Mr O'Connor who used to work at the gallery was gone. He'd retired and lost his mind, hanging imaginary paintings on the walls around his sitting-room before he died. He carried on being mad and his wife went before him. On the morning of her funeral he greeted mourners at the church, confused. 'Doris will be along in a moment,' he told them, 'I can't think what could be holding her up.' Genevieve had made it to the church service but didn't have the stamina to stay for the day. Mrs McCabe was there without her husband, Morris. He'd had a heart attack at the breakfast table one morning, had slumped into his bowl of cereal and drowned. Didi Malone reapplied some mauve eye shadow while talking to Mr Barnham, who was picking candle wax from the centrepiece, looking the way someone does when they have to listen to someone who is unlikely to stop talking for a very long time.

No one spoke of my father's disappearance and no mention was ever made of the book of poetry that was found in his pocket. It was no longer open to speculation; it was avoided in the same way as anything tricky or unpleasant – alcoholism, infidelity, fruitiness – always was. They retold their favourite old stories instead. There would always be the things they chose to see and those they chose not to.

Doctor Long stood by the opened front door, tugging at a cigar. He was fine, he said, eyes raw from smoke and from crying, he just needed some air. Ollie mustered mourners by him at the doorstep, who departed with empty casserole dishes, serving plates and doilies, Mrs Scott Hamilton looking somewhat hurt with an almost full plate of grape and sour cream bites.

My father's death was not the only cause for upset that day; it reminded his friends of their own bereavements, of their own mortality. They got nostalgic about all sorts of things aside from him, especially the men, all sorts of things they could finally get out, things they had been unable to cry about before.

I heard so many stories about father, so many things I'd never known. I wanted to know everything about him, I was hungry for information: what he did, what he liked, everything he was now unable to tell me. I lapped it all up.

It was recounted how, as young teachers, my mother and father had been put in charge of thirty students on a train travelling through Italy. My parents had been having dinner in the dining car, the students in another carriage and asleep, when an announcement was made over the tannoy. There was a redirection point at Lucca, where specific carriages would be uncoupled and sent on alternative routes. My father would have had no difficulty in comprehending the Italian, but he'd been so absorbed with my mother that he had paid no attention to it. While they were on their way south to Florence, warm and woozy, fixed on each other in the light of their tasselled table lamp, their students were headed east for the Balkans.

My father's secretary, whom I'd never met before, was a huge woman in a ballooning, black tent with cropped, purple hair and suede, pointed-toe shoes that wouldn't have looked out of place on an elf. How could my father have tolerated any of this? Was there a quirky side to him that I hadn't known about, a side that fathers' children never see? She told me about the shirt he had spent hours searching for one Christmas – how he had walked all over the city centre, four lunchtimes in a week, how he'd fretted about the colour being right for me.

In bed that night I studied a photograph of my parents: it must have been on their wedding day or shortly after – everyone's dressed up and smiling, there are spots of confetti floating about. My father, dapper as ever, but with a full head of hair, parted far to the side, an earlier model of his tortoiseshell glasses, has his fingers cupped around my mother's waist. They are on their way somewhere; everything is moving, fluid. In a flurry of hats and handbags and faces and fingers, white roses and gloves, is my mother: delicate, smiling, radiant, gazing off into the distance, perfect, proportionate features, luminous eyes, vanilla skin. Look after your mother, someone had said outside the church. She was more beautiful now than she'd ever been.

She knocked on my bedroom door on her way up to bed that night, with her hot milk and water bottle for comfort. I pushed the photograph down the side of my bed, worried that it might upset her. I still couldn't cry. My father was dead. It was too big a thought to think. She leant over me and rubbed my hair, saying nothing, her mantras silenced now, warm tears dropping into my ear.

20

Dragonfly

It was a perfect October day – a July sky without its warmth, puffed up clouds, deep shadows in stark sunlight – that sort of substantial day when you can see your own breath. Everything was clean-edged and sharply defined: dripping ferns, diaphanous spider webs in the light, starlings swooping to pluck worms from sodden soil. All looked new, bright and orderly and in its right place, the way I'd imagined America to be as a child.

The graveyard was deserted, as graveyards always are, its thousand silent inhabitants laid in layers below. There had been a heavy downpour earlier, which left the air rich and damp, petrichor, and the sun's reappearance had created spectrums of colour in potholes. October was the right month for new beginnings, so much better than January when everyone who has held on through Christmas gives up and dies, death notices filling the back page of *The Irish Times*.

In the ten months since my father's death, there had been increasing moments of clarity. There was a sense of space around me. The world felt more organized and I felt safer in it. My mind no longer hurt, the strain had gone; my eyes were wet and opened wide.

I saw not just a tree, but each of its leaves as if through a magnifying glass – the veins and arteries bleeding from the stem, all its shades of colour: black, brown, saffron, wine, red. The shine of chestnuts split from their shells, a single feather lodged like a spear in the ground – Indians hiding in the tree house. The silver trail of a snail on its slow course around a stone plot, dew on an elderly rose. You must deadhead those roses, Mum would say, whipping them off with her hands.

I walked along rows of graves looking for my father's, the soft grass underfoot a thin veneer to what lay beneath. *Taken from us, Dearly Beloved, Rest in Peace.* I passed a large, well-tended plot where generations of a circus family lay buried – the strange talents of a different tribe, the bearded lady, the juggler, the tightrope walker, the contortionist folded in his coffin – and thought of that disastrous outing that had begun as a treat, when our father had taken us to the big top in Booterstown. He had been in mellow humour that day: candyfloss was purchased, we were allowed to scare ourselves by running up the widely spaced wooden planks to the back of the tent.

Our excitement at having front-row seats turned to terror as the ringmaster flicked his whip at some tigers in a cylindrical cage, which wobbled and swayed as they flung themselves against its sides. Above us the huge canvas tent flapped wildly in the wind – the whole structure seemed precarious. My father tried to reassure us but looked ready to make a run for it himself, with his overcoat rolled under his arm. The outing was abandoned – it seemed impossible to keep us happy – we were taken home early, in tears.

It was an easy grave to miss. There was nothing to it, no cross, no picture, no candle, just neat, raked gravel below the plainest headstone in the cemetery – grey, with simple carved lettering; no epitaph. It wasn't at a prominent corner spot, it wasn't out on its own under a tree, my father's body had been packed uncomfortably close to a Mr Boland whose own tomb was of flamboyant black marble and engraved in gold writing, making my father's appear all the more forlorn. Had he been able to move, he would have shifted along for a bit till he found a spot on his own. There was an oblong terracotta pot at its base, holding several smaller plastic flowerpots, all of them empty.

I hadn't noticed how simple it was in all the fuss and flowers from the funeral. The most elaborate of arrangements, wreaths and bouquets had been laid on top of his grave that day, all long gone. The coffin had been lowered respectfully, soil spaded on top, everyone blessing themselves. But between then and now the earth would have become heavy from rain, flattening the box below, splayed limbs poking through splintered wood. I saw the skull beneath the thinning epidermis of his head. I stopped myself.

A bird had left its mark over his name, dried now; I picked at it. From somewhere I could hear laughter.

Smoke rose in twists from a chimney in the distance, clouds moved and climbed. Mountains folded beyond that. Shafts of light behind them, almost biblical in their drama, were charged with a change coming. My eyes were taking me on journeys I had never been on before. The scale of my world was increasing by the moment. My eyes were travelling, like light. If the world didn't curve away from me I felt I could have seen right across it.

I turned to leave. My father was not here. This place was just a set, and I was acting out a scene. Nearby was waste ground, not yet developed; a potter's field. Where the land dropped away, a pond had formed, illuminated by a thin expression of light. Hovering over it was a small thing: a dragonfly, darting erratically as if moving between invisible plateaus in the air.

I saw it clearly, though my eyes were moist, in colour and detail and shape: a lone late dragonfly in the frigid air, battling the winter wind. I thought of my father's letter.

I saw clearly for the first time, a perfect beauty hovering in sunlight over water.

21

Metamorphosis

Its eyes were enormous. Big, beautiful and electric blue. Twenty-eight thousand lenses focusing in faultless vision. Perfect half-circles made up of two sections, one scanning the sky above, the other searching below.

It was in the air at sixty miles an hour. Millions of years ago, when Ireland was south of the equator and beneath a sulphurous sea, dragonflies darted. Their legs like arms, catching, holding and clinging.

The dragonfly began there, below the surface, hatching as a dull-brown predacious nymph absorbing oxygen through gills, growing by a variable number of moults. It lay low in the shadows of the pond for years.

It crawled into the world, beyond the surface, and a metamorphosis began. Released from the grim, grey, myopic, restricted grub life it unfolded into new freedoms and splendour.

The body swelled, the skin split. Blood pumped into new unfurling wings. Strawberry red, acid green.

From the dark it came into the light.

Lucy Bastonme